When the world ended would anyone survive?

"Once upon a time, not that long ago, there was a city called Vancouver, in a province called British Columbia, in a country called Canada. This city had millions of people in it and huge buildings. The buildings were so tall the sunlight never reached the ground; everything was in shadow all day and all night."

I paused to gaze at my audience. Their mouths hung open and their eyes were round with disbelief.

Tales of the Fantastic

RITA Schulz

53RD STREET PUBLISHING

Tales of the Fantastic
Rita Schulz

Published by 53rd Street Publishing at Smashwords

Copyright 2014 Rita Schulz
All rights reserved

Cover image© Unholyvault | Dreamstime.com

This is a work of fiction and purely created from the
authors imagination. Any resemblance to persons
living or dead is purely coincidental

About the Author

Rita lives on the Sunshine Coast in British Columbia with, Russ, her husband, who is also a fiction writer.

She has written for years and is an alumnus of the Oregon Writers Network, and the Greater Vancouver Chapter of the Romance Writers of America.

Her most recently published stories are Fire in Their Hearts with R.G. Hart from Champagne books, and Ladies of the Jolly Roger from 53rd Street Publishing.

Please visit her website at http://www.ritacrossley.com to view her other works.

Table of Contents

Dedication

For Russ for his love and support

And for my friends who never fail to life my spirits
and make me smile.

And for Kris, Dean, Steve, Chris, and Colleen,
this one's for you.

Introduction

I've always loved reading fantasy and science fiction stories, so it wasn't surprising that as I sat down to write short stories, this is where my imagination brought me.

I decided to offer a mixed bag of stories in this collection. Some stories are serious, such as "Once Upon a Time," with a look at a possible future, and two others, "Flower & Bird" and "A Little Kitchen Magic" are urban fantasy. The remaining two, "Blarney" and "Party Central," have a gentler sensibility with a touch of humor.

I hope you enjoy reading these Fantastic Tales as much as I enjoyed writng them.

Enjoy!

Rita Schulz
May 2014

Flower and Bird

HER HAND FOUND NOTHING.

Flower stopped right in the middle of the busy sidewalk and put both of her hands up, feeling along the length of the slender golden chain she wore.

She started to panic. Her mouth went dry and her palms started to sweat.

She took a deep breath and looked down at her feet, then back the way she had come. Nothing.

She was only a short distance from the bank where she worked. That was one good thing about Vancouver Credit Union: there were plenty of branches to choose from in this city.

She continued down Burrard Street, heading north. The air was damp and cold this January morning in Vancouver.

Flower and Bird

The heavy grey sky threatened rain mixed with snow. The normal, breathtaking views of the ocean and mountains were completely hidden under cloud and fog.

Flower turned left on Pender, walking west. A couple of blocks later she came to the two-story cement building with its red Vancouver Credit Union sign.

She hugged her thick, navy blue wool coat around her, trying to keep in as much warmth as she could, but she was still shivering. She wasn't sure whether to blame the cold or the possibility that she had lost her pendant.

She entered through the heavy main doors that were made of special glass with steel push plates. She knew she had to get downstairs into the ladies washroom as soon as she could.

She would check her clothing and coat in case the pendant was hung up in the folds of cloth or the lining.

She shrugged off her coat and draped it over one arm as she walked down the dark cream hallway with its grey-blue floor. It was a conflicted color combination, looking as if the decorator couldn't decide which way to go: cool or warm.

Flower kept walking as quickly as she could, trying not to draw any attention to herself.

She could feel her energy start to drop. It wasn't serious yet. A good shot of blue algae and a couple of mouthfuls of ghost fern would keep her going until she got home.

Of course, finding the pendant would be best.

She felt a brush of cold air against her cheek. The air stirred her long dark hair, which for a moment floated around her head and face like a soft cloud.

Flower couldn't help but shiver, goose bumps rising on her body.

At her locker in the ladies washroom, she dialed the combination and opened the door. The locker was one of the old grey metal varieties that high schools used to use. The only attractive thing about it was that she didn't have to share it with any other staff member at the credit union. She checked the shelf and the bottom of the locker. No pendant.

She was still hoping that the pendant had gotten hung up in her clothing somehow and she would be able to find it.

It was the one-and-only true shade talisman she had. At least, that's what her mother had told her. She had another pendant that would work for a while, but didn't have the complete power that the original one did.

Flower took off her coat and searched it thoroughly, then hung it on the available hook. Then she entered the ladies washroom, quickly pulled off her deep red wool sweater, and checked the sweater and her bra. No, there wasn't any pendant hiding where it shouldn't be.

Flower shivered again, only this time she knew that it was being half naked in the cold basement rooms. The old cinder block walls seemed to trap the cold and never let it go. It didn't matter how much heat they poured into the old basement, it never seemed to warm up.

She re-dressed herself as quickly as she could.

Flower returned to her locker and pulled out a bottle of her special blue algae juice, downed a good healthy mouthful. She winced as she felt it going down her throat. She wanted to rinse out her mouth to erase the awful, bitter aftertaste, but she knew that she didn't have time.

She reached into her purse and pulled out her lipstick.

"What are you drinking?" asked a sharp voice from behind her.

Flower's heart stuttered in her chest and she drew a deep calming breath. Great, just what she didn't need—questions. She had just settled down in Vancouver and wanted to stay in the pretty little city for a while.

"Hi, Mary. You startled me. It's a special blue algae juice. Would you like to try some? It's very good for you. I've been taking it for years."

She knew that it wouldn't hurt a human, not really. Mary, her supervisor, probably wouldn't feel anything at all. Mary didn't look or act like the kind of person who was in tune with her body or mind.

"Healthy eh? Can I see it?"

Flower had hoped that her ploy would work, but maybe that was too much to hope for.

Flower smiled, pulled out the dark blue glass bottle, opened it, and passed it to Mary.

At that moment Flower felt another deep chill, and her toes started to fade. She smiled at Mary and made sure that she didn't look down to confirm the disappearance of her toes. The juice wasn't working as it should, and Flower knew that she had to get home quickly, but she had to get rid of Mary first.

Mary took the bottle and tentatively sniffed it. She wrinkled her nose and passed it back to Flower. Flower knew that she had to act quickly. She had to tell Mary she wasn't feeling well. That she would have to go home right now. She had to hurry—she could feel herself disappearing.

"Actually, Mary, I was taking an extra dose of my algae juice because I wasn't feeling well.

"It's an herbal remedy that usually helps, but it's not working today. I'm sorry."

Mary looked at Flower, nodded, and started to walk away. She stopped and looked back. "Call us if you can't come in tomorrow. Anyone who would drink something that smells like that must be desperate."

Flower watched until Mary, in her worn shiny pants, mismatched blazer, and flat worn shoes, went up the stairs and was out of sight.

Flower quickly closed up her blue algae bottle and put it back into her locker, then pulled out her coat and slipped it over her shoulders. She knew she had to hurry. She would come back and look for her locket tomorrow. Right now she had to get home to her little apartment. She had to stop herself from disappearing entirely.

***

All the way home, Flower felt as if someone or something were following her. She kept turning around and trying to peer through the heavy mist and rain. Vancouver certainly had its wet season. Mind you, that was one of the reasons that she liked it here.

Vancouver reminded her of England, especially the town of Bromley, where she had been born and raised.

"Psst, I see you. Do you see me?" said a soft, echoing voice behind her.

She pulled her coat close to her body, then stopped and spun quickly around to face the person who was following her.

There was no one there.

She thought she heard soft laughter on the wind as it whipped around her, taking her long hair and fanning it out in the rain.

She turned toward home and increased her pace. She wouldn't run, it wasn't dignified. That's what she had always been told. It had been part of her training, her conditioning, as she grew up. But she certainly could do a little speed walking.

Soon Flower put her key into the front lobby door of her three-floor, stucco-and-cedar-sided apartment building. It may have been an old building, as far as Vancouver was concerned, but it was kept neat and fresh. Someone took great care to make sure that the grounds had a nice assortment of evergreen and deciduous trees and shrubs, so there were always some green growing things to welcome people when they came home.

Flower noticed that her left hand was starting to disappear. She needed to make it into her apartment and get some raw ghost fern into her stomach while she still had use of her hands.

Fear clutched at her. She tried to swallow, but her mouth had gone dry.

When she opened the door to her apartment, the tension started to lift from her shoulders. She was home. Help was literally just around the corner.

Flower dropped her coat and handbag on the floor as she walked down the hallway to the kitchen.

She knew that she had a spare pendant that she could use for the time being, but it didn't work as well at the true one her mother had handed down to her.

It wouldn't be the same, of course.

She really wanted to find the antique family heirloom she had worn around her neck since she had been turned into a Shade, but that would have to wait.

Now she had to save herself, before it was too late and she completely turned back into a Shade.

She was a Shade with a corporeal body. She didn't really know how the magic worked, but she knew that the secret had been handed down to the women over many, many generations. It was a small, select family line, originally from the gypsies in Romania.

The original pendant, made by her mother, contained a sample of her blood, dirt from where she had been born, and dirt from where she had been buried.

The spare pendant only had two of the three ingredients and was much weaker. It was fine in a pinch, but she needed the original pendant back to retain her corporeal being.

She felt the familiar tingling that meant that something else was going to disappear, and it was coming from her right hand.

Panic gripped her and she ran for her refrigerator and pulled open the door.

She felt the tips of her fingers start to throb. She reached for the ghost fern juice and made sure that she used the palm of her right hand to twist the cap off

"Oh, please, Oh, please," she whispered.

Flower braced the blue bottle against her left forearm and her right wrist and awkwardly drank. She started to spill in her haste and forced herself to slow down. If she spilled the bottle... She forced the thought away from her mind and concentrated on what she was doing.

She carefully swallowed the juice. She took a couple of calming breaths. It was going to be fine.

The throbbing in her right hand stopped, and then the tingling went away, too.

She carefully put the bottle on the counter next to the refrigerator, then went to sit down at the little white wrought iron bistro table set.

Flower sat with her long, slender legs stuck out in front of her and her arms limply hanging on either side of her.

She slowly lifted her right arm and watched as her hand reappeared. It was working. The juice was doing its job. Her left foot was coming back, as well. It tingled like pins and needles.

She kicked off her boots in the direction of the hall, got up and took another long swig of the juice. It tasted like old socks and ferns, but there were worse things, like turning back into a Shade or a Wraith. No, thank you, she enjoyed the mortal world too much.

"Mother!" Flower yelled as she went into the hallway and picked up her boots. She opened her neat closet and put the boots and her coat away.

As she slid the closet door closed, she felt something on her cheek, like feathers softly caressing her. She automatically rubbed the spot and felt goose bumps running down her spine.

"Mother," she called again.

It wasn't very often that she called her mother.

She couldn't remember the last time they had actually spoken. Maybe her mother was angry at being ignored for so long. As the time went on and her mother didn't answer, Flower started to get worried.

Maybe she should call her Aunt Rose or Aunt Maddie. She sighed as she considered what her best options were. She had to be patient and not panic. The juice was helping so far.

First, she had to get hold of her mother and find out what was happening to her. Second, she had to find out what had happened to her pendant. She knew she hadn't lost it. The clasp was soldered and very strong. The chain was still around her neck, so it hadn't broken.

She felt a soft gust of air and the same little laugh that she had already heard a couple of times today. Only this time she thought she could hear someone call her name. It was so soft it was out of her hearing, just a very faint whisper.

She concentrated as hard as she could on the word "mother" and called: "Mother. Mother. Mother. I'm sorry; it's been far too long since we've visited. Please come."

This would be the third and last time she would call her today. If her mother didn't answer after her third call, she either didn't want to come or couldn't.

That was something her mother had promised her when she was little. She remembered it clearly. She and her sister Bird had been in the garden. It was summer, and they were playing on the old swing that was tied to the cherry tree. The light was dappled, and the sweet fragrance of the roses filled the air.

Bird was six and Flower seven. They were dressed in little shorts and tops their feet were bare. Flower smiled as she remembered the feeling of the grass between her toes.

Her mother had come out of the house holding tall glasses of water, with a slice of sweet orange in each. It was their favorite summertime drink. She sat down with them at the old wooden picnic table and looked at each of them.

"Girls, I want to let you know something. I want you to know that I love you very much and that I will come to you if you call me three times. You must concentrate very hard on me as you do it. Do you understand?" she said.

Mom looked so serious. Bird started to laugh and Flower almost did, too. Mother must have been playing pretend, one of their favorite games. But Flower looked into her mother's dark grey eyes and there was no sign of humor there. She was serious. It scared Flower.

"Bird, no. It's not a game," said Mother.

Rita Schulz

"Silly mommy," said Bird.

Daddy called from inside the house and Mother got up and smiled at the two girls. "Remember: call three times and think hard." Then she disappeared into the house.

***

There were times in the past, not many, when Flower called her mother, and she had always come. And there were times in the past that Flower knew that her mother was going to be coming to visit. It was like a tie, an invisible thread that she knew was there. It didn't interfere with anything; it was just there, and at times she might get a little tug on it, or she might tug it, but usually it was just there.

Flower had one for Bird, too, but it didn't seem that there was anything attached to it. It seemed to be just a loose thread drifting lightly in the wind.

Flower was starting to feel better. She knew that she should retrace her steps from the beginning of the day all the way back to the bank.

She tried to remember the last time she'd had the pendant. She had it after her shower and after she had gotten dressed.

She remembered because she checked on the length of the chain to see if it went with the outfit she was wearing.

Flower heard a tap, tap, tap and then realized what she was doing and stopped. Her index finger was tapping her teeth. It was an old habit. Something she did when she was deep in thought or was worried.

Flower went into her bedroom with its large, dark, four-poster wooden bed and matching mirrored dresser. The bed was done up in a fresh white-and-blue antique quilt and the windows had heavy matching blue drapery. She pulled some fresh clothes out of her dresser and closet, then took off the ones she was wearing.

She examined herself in the mirror. Everything seemed to be back where it should be. She felt relieved.

Flower went through her worn clothing very carefully again, just to make sure that the pendant hadn't got hooked up somehow. It just didn't make any sense; where could it be?

She pulled out her jewelry box and checked her other chains, pretty rings, earrings, and bracelets. She often added some of these to match her outfits. But the chain she was wearing always had the pendant on it. Her mother had told her she must wear it every day and she did. She called it her signature piece.

Flower felt a little mental tug and quickly pulled on the comfortable jeans she had chosen and another soft, deep red sweater that went well with her light grey eyes. She remembered something. She had caught her scarf in her coat this morning as she was getting ready for work. Flower went to the hall closet and checked her coat, but her scarf was gone.

She had started hearing that voice and getting those strange little face brushes at about the same time.

Flower went into the kitchen and put on the kettle. If company were coming, maybe tea would be a good thing.

The intercom rang. She smiled to herself. The tug had gotten stronger and she knew that it was her aunts. She buzzed to let them into her apartment. "Come on up," she said into the speaker as she poured the water into her Blossom Time teapot to warm. She swished it around and poured out the water, then filled it again with hot water. She then dropped some loose tea into a tea fob and plopped it into the teapot.

There was a knock on the door and she went to answer it.

There at the door stood a young woman, tall and slender, with a pretty face. Her eyes though, were a cold, icy blue. They were the kind of eyes that looked right through you, found you unworthy, and dismissed you. And her lips were pencil thin, painted a deep red. The mouth would be best described as cruel.

She wore a lovely thick, black, cowl-necked sweater and the fashionable black slim trousers that all the young ladies would like to wear, but only a few should. On her feet she had a pair of scarlet red leather boots, and she carried a designer hobo bag of black and scarlet leather. She looked tres chic in her thick wool coat, black with red accents.

Flower stood stunned as she looked at her visitor.

"Move aside, sister," said the tall blonde as she pushed past Flower to enter the apartment.

Flower hesitated for a moment and then softly closed the door behind her guest and followed her into the living room.

Her guest stood in the middle of the living room, giving everything a once-over, and judging by the sneer on her lips, finding it severely lacking.

Flower finally found her voice. "Who are you and what are you doing here?"

"Oh my. Is this where you actually live? How quaint, I guess."

Suddenly Flower felt someone violently push her into the wing-backed chair by the front window next to her display of orchids.

She looked around her to see if there was someone

else that she hadn't seen enter.

"Oh my goodness, did Mother not teach you anything? Well, she didn't teach me anything, either. I had to learn everything and figure it all out for myself."

Flower sat, unable to move, listening to the stranger. She thought that not moving might be wisest anyway. The stranger certainly appeared to have pushed her without touching her. Since she didn't know what the stranger was talking about, she didn't really have a response.

It seemed that this was going to supersede her plans to find her pendant.

"Sorry I took your pendant. Actually I'm not, because I did it on purpose. Mother always did like you best, so you have to pay," the woman held up a pendant that looked like the one Flower was seeking.

Flower gave a small cry of relief and automatically reached for the pendant. The woman snatched it away and gave her a cold, thin-lipped smile.

Flower looked at the young woman closely, and then very gently pulled on her sister's thread. It grew taut, something it hadn't done since they were children. Flower sat there stunned as she realized that this total stranger was her little sister. Joy flooded her mind. She had given up all hope of ever seeing her sister again.

"Bird. I can't believe it," said Flower as she stood to give her sister a hug.

Flower was pushed back into the chair, although not with quite as much force as before.

The joy was short-lived as she realized that her mother had told her that Bird was dead. That she had died and would never come home again. So how could she be here now?

"Mother? Where is Mother?" Flower asked, growing suddenly afraid.

This was the first time that her mother hadn't answered her; that had never happened before. Could her mother be gone? Flower felt an icy feeling crawl up her spine.

The door buzzer rang and Flower looked at Bird.

"Maybe that's her now," Flower said. She got up off the chair and headed toward the intercom.

"I'll let you answer it this once, but next time you have to say Simon says, and ask me for permission. Just get rid of whoever it is. We have a lot of catching up to do," said Bird, with a strange smile on her face. Her eyes had a cold, dead quality to them that really scared Flower.

Flower was quickly getting the impression that if this was Bird, something was really, really wrong with her.

Flower knew that she had to get to the bottom of this. She wasn't getting a loving feeling from this person at all.

Flower knew that she was a Shade and that her whole family were Shades. That their existence was very tenuous in this world with their borrowed bodies.

"Sure, Bird I'll do that," said Flower as, turning her back to her sister, she picked up the receiver.

"Hi," was as far as she got. Her Aunt Maddie spoke quickly on the phone. "Flower, make it sound like it's someone asking to be let in from another apartment. Is Bird there?"

Flower felt a sense of relief as she heard Aunt Maddie's voice. Now she had some help.

"Yeah, they do live here. Aren't they answering their phone?"

"Listen, both Aunt Rose and I are here and between the three of us we can take care of Bird. I guess she's there right now?" said Aunt Maddie.

"Yeah, they told me that they were expecting you, but they were having trouble with their phone and the manager is supposed to fix it."

"Let us into the apartment building. Is your door locked?"

"Yes, they left me with their key and told me to let you in.

I'm their neighbor, so come up to the third floor. I'll meet you at the elevator," said Flower as she turned to look and smile at Bird.

Flower leaned around the corner into the kitchen, opened a drawer, and pulled out a key on a fob. She came back into the hallway and swung the key back and forth so that Bird could see it.

"I'll be right back. Got to let a neighbor it," said Flower as she pressed down the phone and turned to her apartment door.

"How stupid do you think I am? You're not going anywhere," said Bird.

Flower stood completely still. Not that she wanted to, but she couldn't move a muscle. She wondered what would happen next. Would she be killed? Would it hurt?

"You really are a slow learner. Read my lips, I told you to say 'Simon says, May I go to the door?'" Bird enunciated each word to such a degree that froth formed at the corner of her mouth.

"Of course. Sorry. Simon says, May I go to the door?"

"Simon says yes, you may."

Flower felt her muscles release and she could move. It took all the control she possessed not to run to the door.

If she did, she knew that Bird would suspect something was wrong. She might be crazy, but it was crazy like a fox.

Flower walked at a normal pace down the hall and heard Bird move to the sliding glass window of her living room.

Flower opened her door and pretended to talk to someone as she let her aunts in. "Do you know their apartment number? Why don't you take it and then you can slide it under my door when you finish?"

She wanted to hug her aunts, but knew that that would have to wait until this was over.

Aunt Maddie was a sweet looking little woman with soft, short, curly brown hair. She was a little on the round side. In contrast, Aunt Rose was a tall, slender woman with a loud voice, who liked to dress in style. It seemed that her hair color changed as often as her outfits did.

They were two of Flower's most favorite people in the world and she had utter confidence and faith in them.

"Hello, Bird," said Aunt Maddie when she entered the room. She watched Bird's back as she looked out the window.

"Hi, Aunt Maddie. Is Aunt Rose here with you too?" asked Bird.

"Of course dear. Now what's going on, Bird?"

"Well, I have kind of a choice. And I can't decide which one would be more fun. Do I take Flower's pendant and put her in Harbor House like you put me, or do I just turn her back into a Shade with no hope of ever being reborn?" said Bird as she turned to face them and moved away from the window.

"I don't understand why you would want to harm Flower? Of all the people in this world, she is the only one who had nothing to do with your incarceration," said Aunt Rose as she moved to stand on the other side of Bird.

"But she didn't come to get me. My own sister just left me there to rot."

Flower took a deep breath, ready to speak in her defense.

"No, that's only your perception. You don't know the facts," Aunt Maddie said as she slowly walked a little closer to the window. She seemed to slip a little as she moved past Bird.

Aunt Rose continued. "She was never told what actually happened to you. Your mother felt it was best that all she was told was that you were gone. She was very young and she believed that you had died. Even the thread between you was loosened so she could not reach you."

Bird watched Aunt Rose with a little smirk on her lips.

Flower realized that the three of them were now circling Bird.

Flower watched as her two aunts took turns in talking to Bird and at the same time tightening the circle until they were within an arm's length of each other.

"Bird, you need to go back," said Aunt Maddie as she raised her hand and took hold of Flower's with one hand and Aunt Rose's with the other.

Flower completed the chain.

She looked at her long-lost sister and wanted to cry.

"Bird, did you indeed banish your mother?" asked Aunt Rose.

"Yes. I took her pendant and smashed it in front of her. I scattered the dirt from her grave into the wind and emptied her blood onto the ground. She's gone."

Flower gasped as she heard what Bird had done. She knew that the dirt might be able to be found if you knew where the person was buried, but the blood taken before death could never be replaced.

Flower watched as Aunt Rose and Aunt Maddie looked at each other, and then they nodded.

"Bird Averill Thompson," Aunt Rose started to speak, then stopped as Bird started to laugh.

"You old fool. You think you're so smart. I killed Mother, and if you don't back off, I'll kill Flower, too." Bird started to walk toward them, her hand going into the pocket of her pants. Then she stopped.

"No, Bird you won't," said Aunt Rose. "I have Flower's pendant and yours as well. You will be going away."

Aunt Rose started again, "Bird Averill Thompson, by the powers that have been placed in us and with heavy hearts, we now sentenced you to Sanctuary."

Bird looked around wildly at them. Her eyes were open wide and it looked like she was trying to scream, but no sound came out.

Flower started to take a step forward, but Bird was gone.

She looked at her aunts and saw the tears in their eyes.

"Where is she? Where's Bird?"

"She's in Sanctuary."

"It's okay. She'll be helped there. Doctors and stuff," she said. But she knew from the looks they exchanged that something else was going on. "Right?"

"No, Flower. She's gone to Sanctuary. It's kind of like a void, a limbo. Very few ever leave there," said Aunt Maddie as she put her arm around Flower's shoulders.

"But why is it called Sanctuary?" Flower asked.

"It's kind of a reverse term. The rest of us have Sanctuary, or a safe haven, from beings who are dangerous and would harm us, or themselves."

Aunt Rose slipped Flower's necklace from her pocket, placed her pendant onto its chain, and then placed the chain around her neck.

As Aunt Rose settled it around her neck and Aunt Maddie whispered blessings, Flower looked at them both. The pain in her chest and head was so great she had to gasp for breath. Then the tears came and with them, grief. She felt like her heart had been torn from her chest and a ball of ice had taken its place. She heard someone wailing and realized that the sound was coming from her own throat.

She had lost her mother and her sister.

Her aunts held her in their arms the same way they had when she was little, and stroked her hair.

When Flower reached for her pendant and wrapped her fingers around it, she remembered when Bird had left the first time.

Flower knew that it would hurt, but that given time it would heal; but first she needed time to grieve for them both.

Once Upon A Time

"ONCE UPON A TIME, NOT THAT LONG AGO, there was a city called Vancouver, in a province called British Columbia, in a country called Canada. This city had millions of people in it and huge buildings. The buildings were so tall the sunlight never reached the ground; everything was in shadow all day and all night."

I paused to gaze at my audience. Their mouths hung open and their eyes were round with disbelief.

My audience was three small children: one little boy and two little girls, not one over the age of six. They started to push each other as they sat under an old blanket in front of the fire.

The others had finished their evening chores and settled in front of the fire as well.

I hoped, by the telling of stories and the singing of songs, that some of the old information would be preserved for future generations.

"Jenna, go on," said one of the little girls as she shoved the little boy, who was trying to get her attention by pulling her blonde braid.

"Yeah, Jenna, go on. By the way, what's a million?" asked my husband Grant in his deep bass voice.

I glanced at him and gave him a smile. He had a way of always making me feel good. I continued my story.

"Do you see the rocks on the hill, and the gravel we climbed to look for the salmon?" I asked the children.

The children nodded at me and smiled. I had their attention again. "Well, there are probably a million rocks there. Do you see the large skeletons of the old redwoods and cedars?" They nodded. "Well, these buildings were even higher than some of them."

I heard the crackle and pop of the dead wood in our fire and smelled the dust and dirt a short distance from the cave we used as a shelter.

I swallowed, but my mouth was so dry that my tongue stuck to the roof of it. I licked my cracked lips anyway to give them a little moisture, but I was left with the metallic taste of blood.

I watched Grant give some water to one of the children, and the other two asked for some, too. I looked at him and handed him my ration. He nodded and smiled at me as he gave them a few swallows each. It wasn't much, but it would have to do.

He returned my water flask and I took a small sip, just enough to rinse my mouth, and slowly swallowed the remaining few drops. I quickly sealed up the flask to make sure that none of the precious liquid evaporated.

We sat in front of a cave in North Vancouver. There was once a temperate rain forest here, but now it was as dry as a dessert. That had been before "The Event," as we called it.

We were fortunate to be living in Vancouver. When the comet hit, it hit one-third of the way around the world, deep into the Atlantic Ocean. It wasn't the original hit that caused the worst damage: it was the aftermath. There were storms, fires, tsunamis, and flooding. The entire planet felt as if it were pitched to one side and shaken, as if a terrier had gotten hold of a rat and was trying to snap its neck. I had been certain that this half of North America was going to break off at some fault line. The entire city had been leveled.

Gone were the impressive tall buildings with their icy glass walls. Gone were the bridges, all fallen onto the ground or into the water they spanned.

The highways and sky train were just partial, twisted pathways going nowhere. All that was left were stumps of a once thriving civilization.

A large percentage of the population had died as each new and more devastating catastrophe had washed the earth clean. Until there was only a couple of handfuls of people left. At least that's all that we had encountered so far.

But as suddenly as it had started, it stopped.

Then it was quiet. Not a sound. No barking dogs, no birds, no cars, no radios. Nothing.

Silence was one of the hardest things to get used to. I had always had background noise around me: the sounds of cars or airplanes, the constant hum of electricity. The quiet was deafening. Luckily I had Grant, and now we had the others. The sounds of their movements helped to ease the feeling that I was completely alone.

Gone were the tall, majestic evergreens and the dense forest floor, covered with fern and salal. Before, the forest had been a place where there was rich spongy soil underfoot and you heard the constant bubbling of ice-cold streams and the piney taste of cool forest air was thick on the tongue and face.

Now everything was dead and dry.

We needed water.

We found shelter when we traveled from South Hill in Vancouver to the caves and canyons of North Vancouver. But we would need a better shelter, a place with water, and somewhere to rebuild.

We had been hit hard in the last three months, but it seemed the situation was stabilized. We hoped.

"Lucy, would you like some help with the children?" I asked as I finished the last of the song requests and put my guitar away.

Lucy was a pretty little Chinese woman who was at the end of her pregnancy. Her belly was large and distended.

"No, I'm fine. It's the least I can do with me like this right now."

There had been only twelve adults we'd encountered as we traveled across Vancouver. We had called out as we went and the dogs had gotten good at scenting and finding people. That's how we had found Kent, a banker in his mid-twenties, and Winston, the little boy. They had both been trapped in rubble, but Grant and I managed to dig them out.

In total we had three women; four if you counted me. I was past childbearing age so I knew that I wasn't as important as the other women. I also looked at my husband Grant. We were traditionalist and our vows meant a lot to each other.

But that was then and this was now. Times had changed a lot of things, but our marriage? I sighed as the hard thoughts and ideas came to me.

In the end that seemed to have been what killed most of the population—being killed immediately, or trapped in the buildings and not able to get out. Then it was lack of electricity, medication, and sanitation. It seemed that for a long time we had one epidemic after another and only the strong and the lucky lived through them.

"Everyone, I think that we need to talk. It's time to have a meeting. Let's say in about ten minutes?" said Grant.

I almost said that most of us didn't have watches since most people used to check their cell phones for the time, but now there wasn't any electricity, the grid was completely down, and it wouldn't be up for a very long time, if ever. But old habits were hard to break sometimes.

Lucy came back from tucking the children into their beds at the back of the cave. It was cooler there and easier to protect them from the predators that had become more and more aggressive.

We had already had run-ins with bears and had a cougar sighting. There were packs of dogs that had quickly gone feral and were getting bolder.

Luckily we found rifles and handguns in the local Gold and Gun store. We had to teach each other how to shoot. "Okay, I'm here. Let's get the show on the road," said Lucy as she carefully lowered herself onto a fallen log that we had pulled over to the side of the fire pit.

I looked at everyone and waited. We had all been talking about what we needed to do to survive.

It was late spring and warm. I wasn't sure if the planet had shifted its axis and we were going to have warmer weather. For all I knew, we had been pushed closer to the sun, but I really didn't think so. I wished I had paid more attention to some of those science and discovery programs when I'd had the chance.

Before the comet hit, we were told that it wasn't as big as the one that had caused the dinosaurs to become extinct. But I wondered how they really knew; after all, they hadn't been here then. It was all a guess as far as I know. These were the same people who'd said we should make sure that we had enough food and water for about a week or two.

Boy, were their estimates off. Or perhaps they downplayed the Event so that people wouldn't panic. People did anyway. When cars plugged up all of the exits out of the city, they tried walking—

and thousands of people were caught out in the open during the worst of it.

"Okay, we need to find water," Kent said as he started the conversation.

"We need a good supply of food. The kids need milk. We have enough powdered milk from the grocery stores to last for a while, but fresh is better," said Lucy.

"I've made up a list of things that we need. It's a long list and includes everything from horses, cows, and goats, to bees and chickens and nuts and seeds. And tools, we need tools too," said Grant as he pulled out a piece of paper from his dirt-crusted jeans pocket.

I nodded and smiled. It was going well. Grant and I had spoken earlier about some of the things that were important to have.

"Bees, what the hell are we going to do with bees?" asked Dorothy, a woman in her early thirties. She had long brown hair the she was now wearing in a long braid. A hairstyle that most of the woman had adopted these days, myself included.

"A lot of things: They naturally will help pollinate the crops for us and will produce honey, probably our only sugar, as well as wax that we can use to make candles," said Grant.

Listening to him made me proud.

He had actually listened to me when we had discussed things that I had been thinking about even before the Event.

No all the people we met or found stayed with us. Some did and others wanted to try and find family or friends. I watched the other women, and Kent the other male. I knew that if we were the only people that were left in this area, we would need to make all the babies we could. We didn't know how the rest of the world fared: there could be pockets where others had survived, but so far it didn't look great for the human race. And the only way to improve the odds of human survival would be to have the most diverse genetic pool that we could. It was long-range planning, but we had to take everything into account.

I felt bile rise up in my throat. I loved my husband, but we were in our fifties. I couldn't help by having children, but he still could. I knew that he took the vows we made to each other seriously, but these were different times.

"Who knows anything about stupid bees?" asked Shirley, a teenage girl from a comfortable gated community.

"I do," I answered.

"It's not the only thing we need. But Jenna and I know a man from our old neighborhood that has the knowledge that we need. He has the farmer and woodsman stuff down pat. He even built his own bread kiln in his backyard. He heated it with wood and it worked perfectly. He grew all his own vegetables and even had a beehive. The food was fresh and delicious. This was all in the city."

I waited for them to reach the only conclusion that they could. I watched as each face reached it.

"Someone is going to have to go into the middle of the city and see what can be saved. There may be other things we can salvage later, but I know where he lives and where the bees are.

"He was alive when we left, but he wanted to stay there, waiting for his children, hoping that they would come home."

I smoothed down my top as I stood and wrapped my shawl tightly around me. My fingers played with the short fringe at the ends and I knew that I was showing my nervousness. The dogs at my feet stood up and stretched. They looked at me, waiting.

"I volunteer to go to South Hill and see what I can come back with. I'll copy the list we have and if there is anything else that we need, that we can't get close by, we'll add it to the list," I said.

I was pleased with myself; my voice was calm and steady even though the acid in my belly was tearing me apart. I looked around the dying fire and looked at everyone in turn and smiled confidently, but I hadn't looked at Grant once.

I had already spoken and discussed this with Grant and Ken and they had both agreed. Neither had been happy with the idea and Grant and I had discussed it until there weren't any more words. All we could do was love each other while we had the time to be together.

"We need you here to help us. And you can't go by yourself: it's too dangerous," said Lucy, looking afraid.

I looked her in the eyes and lied. "Thanks, Lucy. That's sweet of you; it's not that bad. I'll be fine. I won't be gone that long and I bet that I'll be back before that baby of your comes. Okay?"

The odds of me making it back weren't very good. We had had a really difficult time getting here in the first place.

The other two females looked at each other and at Lucy. She and I were the only women experienced in having children, and they were counting on us. But they only needed one, so I was the one that should go. That might make things easier for Grant and the other women.

I kept telling myself I was being logical and making a hard decision for the best interest of the group.

"I'll be leaving as soon as possible. I'll be walking, but I would like to take Buster along with me."

Buster was a large golden retriever and would be good company on the trip. If I was lucky and got some things that were awkward to carry, I was planning to hitch a drag carrier to him.

"You can keep Page." I said to Grant. "She's good at finding and catching rabbits, so you'll have some fresh meat for the pot while I'm gone. And most importantly, I can be on the lookout for water as I travel. I'll make a map and keep a journal about what I find. That way we can use the information when I get back to decide if we should go and where we should go to."

I knew I had them. I had erased any doubts about leaving our little happy group at the mention of water.

I didn't want to go, but I was the best choice—actually, the only choice. I had the best chance of getting there and getting back as quickly as possible while the others took care of the hunting and fishing and protecting the camp.

I watched them as they all started to nod in agreement. We had up to now always stuck together and helped each other; this was the first time our little group was splitting up and no one liked it.

But we needed the information and the bees. It had to be done and they all realized it.

***

I made good time getting out of North Vancouver. While the roads were buckled and the buildings pretty much leveled, it wasn't too bad. I was getting used to it and finding ways around the worst of the destruction. It was still going to be a long journey, probably a good week.

I was lucky and soon found little ponds of ground water to keep Buster and me from becoming dehydrated. I stopped at grocery store that was not one of the ones we were using for supplies and got provisions for the journey.

It really was incredible how everything in the city was so much cleaner than it ever was before the Event. The air was so clear that it was almost painful to look at the horizon. You used to see just a faint outline of the Gulf Islands, but now you could see the shorelines and each island standing out from the others.

At night the sky was so clear and the moon and stars so close that you could almost touch them. The stars high overhead hung in the air like diamonds scattered on a dark blue velvet curtain.

And the moon was a large pale white pearl hanging there, shining gently down on the new world. It all looked so normal, but the stars weren't really in the place that they should be, or that I remembered that they should be. The Big Dipper was there, but it was low on the horizon. I couldn't remember if it was usually that way or if it should be directly overhead. We really needed books from the library: another thing that we would have to do soon.

On the third day of going up Indian Arm, Buster and I found a boat that was still seaworthy and we took it across and entered Vancouver. When we landed, I pulled the boat ashore for the return trip. Buster jumped out of the boat and ran around, then he stopped, stood still, and lifted his muzzle into the air. He moved his head back and forth as he tested the air to locate the scent that had caught his attention.

I heard a deep guttural woof and a heavy shuffling, lumbering sound that didn't belong to any dog I had ever encountered.

It was a bear; I quickly dropped my pack and got my rifle out. It was a light rifle and I knew that it wouldn't do much good in this situation.

"Buster, come here. Stay," I said to the dog in a firm tone.

I knew that the best plan was to get out of the area as soon as possible. I didn't know if it was a sow with cubs or a big old male bear. I knew that their normal food wouldn't be available this year and that would be making them hungry and mean.

I picked up my pack and slung it onto my back as I tried to grab Buster. But Buster saw the bear and started barking; the bear came around the corner of a low wrecked building and charged straight at us. It was a big male and it was mad. I looked around for the nearest building that would give us shelter. It was across a wide expanse of road and rock. I knew we wouldn't make it, but had to try.

I steadied the rifle and quickly fired off two shots and yelled and screamed as loud as I could as I ran toward the bear, waving my arms. Then I stopped and ran the other way still screaming and waving my arms overhead.

My idea of shock and awe didn't work and the bear didn't turn away. Instead he stood up on his hind legs and roared and he swiped his lethal front paws at us.

"Come on, Buster, run!" I yelled at him as I led the way across the road.

He didn't follow me.

I heard a combination of roaring from the bear and frenzied barking and growling from Buster.

I glanced over my shoulder as I ran. Buster was playing a dangerous game with the bear. He ducked between the bear's paws, snapped his teeth, and then ran away. He managed it a few times and then I heard a loud, horrible yelping and a howl of pain.

I got to the building, stopped and turned to look at Buster, and raised my rifle. I couldn't shoot; the bear had him against his chest between his front paws. Then I saw it drop Buster, lift a paw, and rake its claws down his side. I watched Buster go limp, his head hanging to one side, and I knew that he was dead.

The bear picked Buster up, shook him again, dropped him, then turned and headed toward Burnaby, the next town to the east.

Buster had saved me. Tears filled my eyes and I started to sob. I leaned against the building and swallowed hard, trying to catch my breath. I couldn't believe that Buster was dead. It had happened so quickly. He was a brave dog, a good dog, and I would miss him. I started to cry again, and rubbed my eyes hard with my hand.

I was all alone.

I had no one to even talk too, but I couldn't stop. I knew that people were waiting for me and I had to press on. If this mission were to be successful, I would have to keep going while there was daylight.

I started walking again.

The following day, the fifth, I got to Knight Road and followed it all the way to South Hill and to my old home. It was so strange, walking in the old neighborhood, a place that was so familiar and now looked so different. The worst was the smell. The sewage system must have broken, and there was no one to take care of the bodies of the people and their pets.

I heard the yowl of feral cats and saw a small pack of midsized dogs, but they stayed away from me. I knew that I had to be very careful. Individually they were fine, but as a pack they could easily take down and kill a person.

I looked up and saw smoke coming from the back of old man Kurt's place, and I smiled. My trip was not a waste. Now all I had to do was to convince him to come with me.

His knowledge and experience in the old ways of growing crops and taking care of animals could mean the difference between our survival and the extinction of the human race. I felt that with him we had a chance, a good chance.

I went around the side of the house and stepped over the fallen wooden fence that used to separate his property from his neighbor's.

There was no one there anymore so it wasn't needed.

"Kurt, it's Jenna, your neighbor from across the street."

I waited. There was no sound, no answer.

"Kurt. Are you home?" I called again.

"Ya. Come on," said a weak, trembling voice.

I heard the bark of a dog as I came around the corner of the ruined house. There was a tan shepherd looking warily at me. It's barking became frenzied. I froze.

"Kurt. You got yourself a dog?"

He had never had the time for dogs, preferring cats as company.

"Lucky. Enough," said Kurt.

The dog quieted and I moved forward.

I found Kurt. He was lying on a sleeping bag under a tarp that he had strung between four tall logs. It looked kind of like a teepee. He looked very old and grey. His eyes were sunken and bloodshot.

I was shocked and upset at the change in him, but I knew that I couldn't let it show. We really needed him.

"What happened, Kurt?" I asked as I knelt down beside him.

"Well, it's like I say. You never know, do you?"

I leaned over and felt his forehead. He didn't have a fever.

"No, it's my heart. No more medicine," he said.

"I'm waiting for the kids. They should be home soon," he mumbled to himself. "Everything's gone. They're all dead, you know."

"Kurt, I'm going to make you some tea from foxglove. Okay? We'll try it weak first."

"I don't have any."

"No, but I do in my old yard, and so do the neighbors. I saw it as I was coming here. How are you fixed for water?"

"Got plenty in the garage."

I busied myself and got some of the plant leaves from next door and a fire going in his fire pit. I filled the cast-iron pot he had on a three-legged iron stand and left it to boil. Then I pulled a cushion from the swinging couch and put it next to the fire so I could keep an eye on Kurt.

Lucky settled down and soon she was following me around. I took a quick look to see what Kurt had in his garden. After the foxglove tea, I knew that I could make a nice vegetable soup with the fresh tomatoes, beans, and garlic chives he had growing. He even had a small patch of corn and I pulled a couple of ears off to roast on the fire.

"Kurt, we need your help. We need to find water and learn about bees and growing crops. There are about a dozen of us in the foothills of North Vancouver," I swallowed hard. "We can start again, but it would be easier if we had help."

During the next few days I watched him and waited.

During these times I've seen amazing things and sometimes people will rally if they have a reason for going on. But it didn't happen. I was surprised; I would never have thought that Kurt would give up. Maybe his heart couldn't be helped with the simple tea we had.

I needed to make him realize how important he is to us.

"We'll take our time and you'll get stronger."

He looked me in the eyes and shook his head. "Listen. You'll be fine. I have books. Take them, but please leave a note for the kids. They'll be home soon." His voice drifted off.

Me? Who was he kidding? I didn't know anything, not like he did. He had the knowledge and the practical experience. He was the valuable one.

I slowly realized that if Kurt was valuable with his old knowledge, maybe I was too? There wasn't anyone else but me to pass on the survival knowledge.

The thought terrified me.

I knew that I couldn't do it alone. I took a deep breath and felt a calmness and strength come over me.

A short while later he patted my hand as his eyes slowly closed and one last, long sigh escaped from his lips.

I knew he was gone.

I cried for a long time. He was a good man and I didn't know what to do. It would take me hours to bury him and it seemed almost pointless with all the other dead in the city, but I didn't want the animals to get him.

I walked over to the beehive that he kept by the side of the garage, with its partially caved in roof, and looked at it. It was quiet. I waited for a few minutes to see if any bees would come out or go in. Not a bee in sight at the hive.

I had really hoped that Kurt would be able to help us. I didn't know what to do now. Grant and I were the oldest people in our group and we had very little experience with raising vegetables or fruit. But Kurt was a wise man and he seemed to think that I could do it. I would have to give it my all, and I would.

I looked around the yard and found a long cement structure that was low to the ground. It was about four feet high and had a cement floor with an area for drainage.

I realized that this must be the start of a new building or experiment that Kurt was doing, but I saw that this would be a perfect place for his body. I could use some of the metal roofing that had fallen down from his garage for its roof and then I could weigh it down with some heavy rubble to keep out the animals.

It took a while to get everything ready, but finally I went back to get Kurt's body. When I was finished, I said a few words and a small prayer. I knew he would have liked that.

I was tired, very tired, bone tired. I sat down in the shade of the garage. Lucky came and sat a short distance from me and watched me. Books. Kurt said he had books. I knew that he would also have seeds that would help. I wouldn't be going home empty-handed.

I slept for a long time. It was a very deep and restful sleep. As I woke I stretched my whole body from my fingers to my toes; it felt good.

The sun was warm and a gentle breeze tickled my face. It was so relaxing with the sun, the breeze, and the drone of bees in the background. It was a lovely morning.

My eyes snapped open and I made sure that I didn't move.

Bees. I saw one slowly fly by me. Okay, they were bees, but were they the right kind?

I got up and followed the little fellow to a small hive about the size of a grapefruit, between the branches of a tree a short distance from the old hive.

I carefully looked at the bees coming from the hive and then went to the old hive. They certainly looked the same. I knew that if the old queen died, the hive would move with a new queen. These bees had the same markings as the dead ones around the old hive, so I knew that it was worth the risk and trouble of moving them.

Kurt had had a small, light, wide wooden cart in the back of the yard and I had seen that it was still there and seemed unharmed.

I emptied the old hive of the little bodies, but kept the honeycomb. I hoped that the heat and lack of water when the comet hit had killed them, not some pre-Event virus.

I got the cart pulled up to the old hive and loaded it. I went to Kurt's greenhouse that was covered with a light, clear plastic tarp and looked in his garage and workshop. He had cleaned up and repaired a lot of the damage. I found books on topics that wouldn't be in modern libraries or bookstores.

I smiled to myself. These were books with basic, old-time knowledge, written simply, beautifully illustrated, and easy to follow.

I found a length of rope and managed to leash Lucky to the cart. She didn't take much persuading after I gave her a drink of water and some food. She was a docile female and a nice little girl despite the earlier growls. I was very pleased to have a new companion and protector.

I wasn't sure how to move the little hive. Then I remembered that Kurt had bees shipped to him once in a small wooden box about the size of the old-style matchboxes. I needed to find something that would let the air in, but would keep the bees contained.

I carefully went up the back stairs into the remains of the house. One side had completely collapsed, but the other side that had the chimney and the stairs to the basement and the second floor was still standing. I found a piece of cheesecloth in the basement that I hoped would do the trick.

Kurt's house had held up better than most of its neighbors after the earthquakes and fires.

The fire ravaged some areas and left others untouched. Some blocks were completely blackened and flattened and others not so bad. A few small areas had a house or two that you might be able to live in, but there was nothing around and no sewage or electricity.

I loaded everything I could find that would be of use and would fit into the small cart.

49

Lucky and I headed out the next morning at first light. I left a couple of notes for Kurt's children. That way, if they ever did come home, they would be able to find us.

There was still a lot at Kurt's place that we could use and a lot of information in the old-fashioned books I had to leave behind, but I could only take so much with me. When I got back, the group would have to decide whether or not someone should make this dangerous trip again. We would make that decision together.

I was pleased with what I was coming back with, but it didn't really solve the problem of water. We needed a sustainable water supply.

***

I entered the area below our cave site and looked up at the mountains. It did feel like I was coming home. It was amazing that in the few months after the Event, sprigs of green were starting to break though the ground.

Fireweed. That's what would grow first, and then other plants would follow. Good old Mother Earth would be fine.

It was getting to be dusk.

I stopped to watch the western sky turn from the bright blue of the day to pink and purple. Were those wisps of cloud? Might the rain return?

I heard the children before I saw them and they came scrambling toward me asking for a story. I laughed at their excitement.

Then came Grant, with his arms wide open. He held me close and kissed me hard. I felt like my heart was going to break. I knew that I would have to make sure he did what we needed for the survival of people.

"I've missed you so much," he said through his tears. "Who do you have with you?" he asked to distract me as he looked at the dog.

Kent came up and gave me a quick hug too and took the cart.

"This is Lucky. She was with Kurt. He's dead. Buster died, too. But I got bees, a hive, a whole bunch of seeds, and books on all different topics. I'll tell you all about it," I said as we walked the rest of the way to camp.

"Good, you did really well. I was worried."

I nodded. I didn't really know what to say to him.

I walked into the camp and quickly kissed and hugged everyone. Then they left us alone so that we could have some time to ourselves.

We walked past the cave to a small flat rock. We sat in silence, just holding hands and looking at each other until it was so dark we couldn't see anymore.

"I've been thinking," he said.

I waited for him. I knew that this was going to be an important talk.

"I want you to trust me and I want to talk to you about two things. One is water. Do you remember the old stories Kurt used to tell, about his father finding water for the neighbors and how he did it a couple of times, too?" Grant slipped a forked-shaped tree branch into my hands. "I think it's willow, but I'm not sure."

"Oh, come on," I started to say and then stopped. I felt a strange, light pull toward the ground when I slipped both my hands on the short sections of the branch. Strange, I'd have to take a closer look at it tomorrow; it was worth further exploration. But not today, not when I could relax in Grant's arms for the first time in two weeks.

I could tell from his eyes that he was serious.

"The second is more important. You and me. I've been giving it a lot of thought and I think that I can help out and "do my duty" as they say, but still keep our commitment to each other. I think that we can accomplish both if we use some modern conveniences."

Now I noticed a bright glint in his eyes and a smile trying to break free around his mouth and he pulled out a turkey baster and handed it to me.

I looked at him speechless.

"You tell me that artificial insemination works really well for the birds and the bees. Well, how about people? I know it's been done."

I started to laugh.

I knew that he was serious, but it was so ridiculous. It was also worth a try—both that and the dowsing were worth a try.

Just then I heard three little voices chanting louder and louder.

"Once upon a time. Once upon a time."

I knew that I was being called and I had to answer.

Grant and I went to the fire pit and found comfortable seats.

I began my story for the evening.
"Once upon a time there was a man named Kurt..."

Blarney

SHEILA PAUSED IN FRONT OF THE HOUSE and looked at it with a critical eye. She really loved the old, beat-up place.

In the morning mist, it had a charming, quaint cottage look to it. A person could hardly see the holes in the roof, the crumbling chimney, and the disrepair around the property.

It was the poor excuse of a legacy her father had left to her and her mother. But this was what they had to survive on so they would have to make the best of it.

She had decided they needed to make a plan. They needed the Blarney Stone B & B for their livelihood. Running it was the only thing she and her mother really knew how to do. She might be able to get another job doing something else, but she couldn't—and wouldn't—leave her mother alone.

If the Blarney had been in Cork, Ireland, in the shadow of Blarney Castle where her parents came from, it would be doing fine.

But they'd moved to Canada and were set up on the outskirts of Surrey, B.C. amidst withered, wild grass meadows and in the shade of mountains covered in dead pine trees. True, they had a huge chunk of property, but it had nothing on it and there was no reason for tourists to come. The area was definitely not a tourist destination, but that was exactly what they needed.

It was her dream to build this into a beautiful place, with cozy little cottages, beautiful lakes and meadows, and magical fairy woods—a place that people would want to visit again and again.

Sheila gazed at the cottage, reminding herself to call it that; the tourists liked it. She pulled out her brand-new digital camera and took some pictures.

It was a perfect day for photographs, with the sun shining and the soft breeze playing with the clumps of shamrocks in pots along the doorway, and red, blue, and yellow wildflowers in the front of the cottage scenting the air. You could almost imagine fairy's playing amongst the flowers as you waited to hear the sound of a leprechaun's hammer so you could catch him and demand his pot of gold.

Angus, their large, black cat, wandered along the path that led to the front door, painted a shiny bright red. He flopped down in front of the door and looked back at her as if to say 'okay, take my picture.' It was a lovely picture, so she quickly took a couple of shots with her brand-new, top of the line camera and continued around the property, trying to get some good pictures for their website.

She took some pictures of the backyard too, and the little porch she had just finished setting up with a little table and chairs under the large hawthorn tree next to the creek.

There were a few outbuildings on the property that had slowly fallen in disrepair. She stopped at the old, red barn.

It had been a cow barn at one time. It still had a hayloft on top, with a wide, breezy center walkway and stalls on each side. The barn was one of her favorite places. It was at the back of the property next to a large weeping willow, and the stream passed by here, too. She stopped as she heard the light tap, tap of a small hammer.

"Sheila, what're you doing?" asked Patrick, the old man who had rented their barn.

"Ma and I have to get more clients for the B & B, so I thought I'd update the pictures on our website."

She replied. "What are you up to?"

"Oh, you know, just working," he said as he lifted up his shoemaker's hammer and continued hammering away. He was a very small man, with long hair that curled around his collar. He was in his usual attire: a worn old cap and dirty work pants covered by a leather apron.

The smell of hay and leather enveloped her. These were comforting scents to her that she'd known since she was a little girl

Sheila lifted her camera to her eye and took a couple of quick shots of Patrick at work.

"Whoa, Sheila girl, what do you think you're doing? I did'na say you could take me picture," Patrick said as he stomped toward her, holding out his hand. For a little man, he really had a strong presence, especially when he had something to say.

"Please, Patrick. Mom and I need all the help we can get. We need more customers into the place, and you looked so good in the barn, swinging your hammer—so Irish. Please?"

Patrick glared at Sheila. He knew what she said was the truth, but he couldn't agree with her. If he did, his secret would be out and people would be coming, not to visit the B & B, but to capture him.

"No, Sheila girl, I would, but I can't. I need you to delete the pictures," he said as he waited for her to do that.

She gave in and deleted the pictures. "Fine, they're all gone."

"Harrumph," he mumbled; then he turned away and went back to his work. She could hear the tap, tap, tap of his hammer as he continued working.

Sheila had to get back to the cottage to give her mother a hand.

They had been fortunate last night and had had a guest, but only for one night. That meant that the room would have to be cleaned and linens stripped. Then she would gather and place fresh flowers in the six bedrooms and the living room. That was the part she liked best.

As she left the barn and was walking past the willow, she turned around and took a couple of quick pictures. Mostly of the barn and stream, but a couple had Patrick in them, too. She had deleted the first pictures and in these you couldn't even see his face. She was sure that they would be fine to use.

Her mother came into the kitchen as Sheila entered the room. She already had her old-fashioned apron tied around her waist and her long brown hair done up in a loose French knot.

She was a pretty woman in her mid-fifties, tall and slender, with large, almond shaped grey eyes and just a trace of a soft Irish accent.

Sheila gave her mother a quick hug and kiss on the cheek. "Sheila, thank you, but what was that for?"

Her mother, Megan, fondly smiled down at her daughter, Sheila was twenty-five and hadn't reached the same height as her mother, but was still a tall girl at five feet seven in her stocking feet, and had the same slender figure. She had inherited her father's curly, dark red hair and green eyes, and had a smattering of freckles on her nose. Freckles that Sheila would dearly love to get rid of.

"Nothing much, Mum. It's a beautiful day," said Sheila as she opened the large guest book that was on a desk just outside of the kitchen area in the entryway by the front door. She looked at their bookings for the next two weeks. The pages were empty. Things were worse than she first thought.

"Mum, we don't have much to do right now so I'd like to talk to you about an idea I have. I'd like to update our website with some new pictures. I've started taking them already. I need a couple more images: things like you in the kitchen, and Gilley in the entryway greeting guests.

At the sound of his name, Gilley, the fellow who helped around the house, popped up from the front room.

"Good morning, Gilley. You did a lovely job of cleaning the fireplace and the living room," said her mother as she smiled at the tiny man.

"Thank you. Oh, by the way, I came across this and thought you'd like it," Gilley handed her mother a pretty yellow-and-green scarf.

Gilley was a short man, but very stocky and strong. He had unusually long arms and a smooth, bald head. He wasn't swayed by fashion and wore a combination of castoffs that seemed to be comfortable. He wore whatever he wanted, as long as it was clean.

He had been with their household since her parents had come from Ireland. He had always worked in their home as a jack-of–all-trades and handyman. Sheila knew they couldn't have done without Gilley, especially these last five years since her father was no longer with them.

"Thank you Gilley, and how are you today?" asked her mother as she was looking through the pantry.

"Fine, Missus, just fine. Top of the mornin' to you both and what a lovely mornin' it is." Gilley pulled an old stogie from his mouth. Unfortunately, Gilley was always sucking on a disgusting old cigar.

When Sheila was a little girl, she would plan that maybe one day she would sneak up on Gilley when he slept and steal that putrid old thing from him. But she never did. He had always been there for her as a friend and a confidant.

This was her home and she had been raised here. She'd gone to elementary school and high school from this house. Her nearest friend had been Brenda, who lived in town, a couple of miles away.

But she had heard, on more than one occasion, guests complaining about the smell that came from Gilley and his old stogies. She wondered if there was something else that they could give him in its place?

"Actually, Gilley, I'd like to sit and talk with the both of you about our problem." Sheila said to him and her mother. "Let's sit down and see if we can come up with some ideas to improve this place."

Her mother and Gilley looked at each other and realized that she was serious.

"Fine, dear. Whatever you say," said her mother. "I'll put on a pot of tea and maybe Gilley would like a little fresh milk?" Her mother pulled a pot from a gleaming white cupboard and put the kettle on to boil.

"Aie, that would be lovely Missus," he said as he stood in the kitchen.

"Please Gilley, let's sit down at the table. I'll get a pad of paper and we can jot down some ideas on how to get the Blarney back on track and making money," said Sheila.

Soon there were sitting around the large, square, old, oak table that was in the center of the large, airy kitchen, with its gleaming white cupboards, white appliances, bright blue curtains, and grey floor. It was a bright, comfortable, functional room that had always been the focus of the home.

"Okay, the way I see it, we need to attract more guests and they need to come back and, most importantly, we need to have them tell their friends. It's called referrals," said Sheila enthusiastically.

She looked at her mother and Gilley, who sat and watched her with blank looks on their faces.

"I think it's fine. Just us. Good," said Gilley with a wide grin at her as he sipped his milk.

"Gilley, we need more people so that we can make more money. We need money to fix the place up and to pay our bills," said Sheila slowly. She looked at her mother for support, but realized that her mother was looking out the window at a robin on the plum tree in the backyard. Sheila realized she wouldn't be getting any help from either of them.

"Okay, first I'm going to download the new pictures of the house and the barn onto our website. I'm also going to announce a free night's stay to the first person who contacts us. It will only be good for tonight. That should create a little buzz, as they say."

Well, that went better then she had hoped; they may not have any good ideas, but as long as they were willing to work with her, it should be fine.

"Gilley, I have something for you," she said just before he left the kitchen. She pulled out a cardboard box of suckers that they kept on hand for children, if they ever had any, and gazed at Gilley.

"How would you like to trade me a sucker for your stogie?"

"Is this pay?" asked Gilley, very concerned, looking down at his feet and the two mismatched socks he wore.

"Oh, no Gilley, we would never pay you—you're like family. This is a trade. I get to keep your cigar and you get a sucker every day. I'll keep your cigar safe in this box. Okay?" Sheila waited. She knew that she couldn't rush Gilley. This had to be his decision or he would just keep on taking it back, and then he might even try and light it.

"Okay," he said as he reached for a green sucker from the box.

His thick, long fingers quickly took the plastic wrap from it and he popped it into his mouth. "Good," he mumbled around the candy.

Next Sheila studied the comment cards they had received from the few guests that they had had over the last couple of months.

"Mum, I need to ask you something. I've been checking and it seems there have been complaints from our guests about missing scarves and socks. Do you know anything about it?"

"No dear. You know I've always told you to make sure your socks, mittens, and scarves are put away. They're so easily lost. That's probably what it is with the guests, too."

Sheila knew that, but somehow it still sounded funny. But she couldn't quite put her finger on why.

***

"Mum. Sheila! Come quick. Something's wrong. Patrick is gone." Gilley entered the kitchen in a panic.

He had just returned from going to have lunch with Patrick as usual, but still had his lunch bag in his hand.

"What are you talking about, Gilley?" asked Megan as she and Sheila came from different parts of the house.

"I found a note. But I can'na read it. Patrick's gone." He handed the note to Megan.

"Oh, dear me. How could this have happened? 'We have your leprechaun, and if you want him back, give us his pot of gold'," read her mother.

"What a load of junk. It must be kids playing a joke." Sheila shook her head at how silly some people can be.

Her mother looked at Gilley, who looked back at her and sighed. "I need my stogie. You hav'na told her?"

"No, her father was supposed to take care of that, and since then there was never really the right time," her mother said, as she looked very ashamed of herself.

"Tell the girl and then we have to find a way of getting him back. How could this have happened?"

"Sheila, when you said you posted new photos of the old place on the website, did you have any of Patrick?" her mother asked.

"Yes, but you couldn't actually see him. Not his face, anyway. Just a shot of the old barn and him working."

"So your new camera could take a picture of him? I'm shocked," said her mother, her brow wrinkled as she took this information in.

"Poor Patrick," sighed Gilley. "I'll miss him."

"What are you talking about? Have you lost your minds?"

"Child, I need you to sit down."

Sheila was stunned by the soft tone and the words her mother was using. She hadn't been spoken to like that since she was a very small child.

"Now I'm going to tell you something that you will find hard to believe. Bear with me. Do you remember the old tales that your father told you as a young girl of leprechauns, brownies, fairies, and elves?"

"Of course," said Sheila, not liking where this was going at all. "And don't tell me they're true. Tell me anything else but not that..."

"...they are completely true," finished her mother for her. "I think I know a way to get him back. But it will be dangerous. When is the next full moon?"

Gilley went to get the calendar with that long awkward stride of his, and Sheila really saw him for the first time in her life.

"Mother, please. What's going on?"

"Your father had hoped by going back to the Fairy Court we would be protected and no one would find us. But everything has changed," said her mother in a tone of voice that Sheila had never heard before.

"The Fairy Court? You have lost it. Totally lost it."

Sheila shook her head as she backed away from her mother and Gilley. She had to get out of here and get help. Who could she go to? The police? The hospital?

"Listen ta me, girl. Try not to be feared. What your ma says is true. I know that it's going to take you time," Gilley said calmly. "But, please, we need you ta pull yerself tegither an' help us.

"What are you thinkin' Missus?" he asked her mother, who was pacing around the kitchen.

"Ma, you're scaring me. Please, can you put a pot of tea on, or something?" begged Sheila, trying to grasp at something normal.

"The next full moon is another gathering of the good folk in our far meadow. It'll be the summer solstice and The Fairy Court will be in session."

"How do you know?"

"That's what the robin was telling me this morning. It was word from your father."

"But Father is dead," said Sheila, who was now beginning to feel dizzy.

"No, child. We told you he had gone away, and he has. Have you ever wondered why sometimes, especially when you were young, your dreams of him were so vivid? They weren't dreams. He came back to see you twice."

Her sense of reality had been tested to the limits and her mind was starting to shut down. None of this could possibly be real. Maybe she was really lying in a hospital room and the person who needed help was her and not Mum and Gilley. She felt dizzy and had to hold on to the kitchen table.

"Sheila, we need you to take pictures with your new camera. Pictures of the King and Queen, and their court, then we'll trade them for their help to free Patrick. I don't know any other way to get him free, because we can't give the kidnappers the gold they demanded. We don't have any. So they will kill him. But the King and Queen would be able to use their magic and rescue him. Even then he will have to leave us. It wouldn't be safe for him here any longer."

"Gilley, the date?" asked her mother as she turned to face Gilley.

"Tonight, Megan. It's tonight." Gilley looked from Megan to Sheila.

"Good—the faster we act, the sooner we get our friend back. Sheila, why don't you lie down for a while? If you have any questions, and I know you will, I can answer them later. I'll call you in a few hours and we'll have a late supper. Then we'll go over our plan for tonight."

Megan stood and smoothed her daughter's hair and kissed the top of her head like she had done since she was young.

Sheila couldn't rest as she tried to put her questions and feelings into perspective. Far too soon she heard her mother calling her and knew it was time to face her fairy tales.

Her mother had donned a light, quilted jacket with an array of scarves of different colors sewn onto the hem and sleeves that floated around her. It gave Sheila the impression that a bouquet of flowers, gently moving in the breeze, surrounded her mother.

Gilley had his normal, simple clothing on, but he had taken care and found two socks of the same color.

They were waiting for her as she entered the kitchen. She had on her normal attire of blue jeans, a simple tee shirt, a light cotton jacket, and her camera in a leather case around her neck.

"Here, daughter," said her mother as she handed Sheila a lovely, long shawl that had all the colors of the rainbow in soft, fluid shapes. It was the most beautiful thing she had ever seen. She held it up to the light and the colors seemed to shift and move as the shawl moved, flowing like a living thing. She gently draped this treasure around her shoulders.

"We must be going," said Gilley, leading them outside. To Sheila's surprise, there was a small, dun-colored pony and a wooden cart.

"Climb aboard," said her mother as she got into the cart next to Gilley.

"Where did the pony and cart come from?" asked Sheila as she sat next to her mother. She felt the cart shift under her and hung on to the sides.

"Oh, I borrowed it from Robbie down the lane," said Gilley as he clicked to the pony and off they went.

Surprisingly, it didn't take them long at all to get to the dusty, dead meadow. At least that's what should have been there, but tonight it was a beautiful lush meadow, with the silver sound of streams and the fresh scent of thick ferns, wildflowers, and dense green woods.

Finally Sheila pinched her arm. No, nothing, except it hurt. It wasn't a dream?

As they entered the meadow, she heard the sound of laughing people and saw lights twinkling a little way off.

They followed a path that wound through the field until they were at the center of a gathering. There were long tables covered in brilliant white linens and platters and platters of food, anything and everything you could imagine.

There were silver and gold serving bowls of incredible size, brimming full of drink and nectars of every kind. Young men and women were wandering around serving food and drink to the most beautiful people that Sheila had ever seen.

They were without blemish and each perfect; the most beautiful and radiant were sitting in the center under a massive hawthorn tree.

Sheila scanned the crowd, hoping that she would find her father. But she realized she had a more important role to play: taking some good pictures of the King and Queen so they could trade them to free Patrick.

At first she kept between her mother and Gilley, but then her confidence grew and she went out a little distance from them. She made sure that she went behind trees to take her shots and was very careful with her flash. Her camera was wonderful in low light so that wasn't a problem since the twinkling lights made it seem like it was early dusk.

After each careful shot, she made sure to hide the camera behind her shawl and move to another place.

Numerous times she was offered food and drink, but she heeded her mother's warning and made sure she didn't take anything.

Finally, she went off to one side and checked her pictures. They were far better than she had thought. She could hardly wait to download them onto her computer.

Then she heard a loud thumping, three times, and then the sound was repeated. This was followed by the sound of trumpets. Again, three times, a pause, and then three more blasts.

"Approach, Sheila, daughter of Aaron and Megan, and state your request," announced the liveried herald.

Sheila was shocked when she heard her name being called. Her mother hadn't said anything about her doing any talking. This must be a mistake.

She heard her name called again and knew she would have to answer the summons. She looked for her mother and Gilley, but couldn't see them anywhere.

She stepped out from behind a large cedar tree and approached the royal couple. She tried to remember how people curtsied in the movies. She had never really seen anyone do that in real life and she was pleased when she didn't fall over.

"I beg your pardon, your Royal Highnesses. I'm completely new to this court and not sure of the polite way to do things, so please forgive my ignorance. I am here today to ask for your help to free a friend, Patrick the Leprechaun.

"He's been kidnapped from our home and is being held for ransom, by people unknown to us. I beg that you would find him and return him back to our home. Thank you."

Sheila stood still, not knowing what else to say or do. So she waited.

"No," the man sitting on the throne finally said. "Next."

Sheila sighed. She had hoped they would agree to her request without her having to pull out her pictures.

"Okay, may I rephrase that request? Please find and release my friend Patrick, and while you're at, it heal our land and make us a profitable B & B. Before you say no again, I should tell you that I have a number of pictures of you and your court that I will happily place on the web. I figure it will make a great advertisement for our B & B—The Blarney Stone."

Thinking it was time to go for broke, she added, "Oh, and you can release my dad, my mother, and Gilley while you're at it, too. What do you say?"

She couldn't believe that she managed to say all that without stuttering or breaking into a sweat. She made sure that she had a strong hold of her camera. She had the feeling that it was going to be the only way they were going to get out of Fairyland alive.

"Yes, I can see that you are your father's child. What do you mean, you have pictures of us? That can't be done," said the Queen.

"It's new technology. I will show you as long as I have your word not to touch the camera."

Shelia walked forward and bowed again; then she pulled the camera forward so the Queen could see it, though it was still around her neck, and she showed them the pictures.

"How delightful. Is that what I look like?" the Queen asked with wonder in her voice. "I'm beautiful."

Sheila wondered if their reflection showed up in mirrors or not, but she didn't really have time to ask.

"Indeed you are, my Queen," Sheila said, heartily agreeing.

"I must ask you to destroy all your photographs of us," the Queen said, more a demand rather than a request.

Sheila took a deep breath and summoned her courage. "And my request about my parents, Patrick, Gilley, and the Blarney Stone?"

The King looked at her, and then at his Queen, and Sheila saw silent communication pass between them.

"Yes, your requests will be granted, except for this meadow and forest. It will continue to look like an old, uninteresting meadow to mortal eyes.

"We will keep that as ours, to use as we see fit. Do you agree?"

Sheila looked around and saw her father, her mother, and Gilley come out from behind the thrones.

"If I may, I would like to honor my agreement with you, my Queen and King, and stay here with you as Prince of this realm as long as my family is kept safe in the human world, but with the provision that I be allowed occasionally to visit my family," said my father as he looked at Sheila. She saw the love in his eyes and the pleading for understanding.

"Might I also be allowed to visit you here? I would like to know about your history and my birthright," asked Sheila.

Sheila knew that she had them over a barrel with the photographs. If they got out into the mortal world, proving the reality of the Fairy Court, it would damage their current existence. All the humans would be trying to find them and their peaceful existence would be finished. But it cost her, too; if she could keep the photographs and put them on their website, she knew that their little B & B would be full every day for many years.

The King and Queen smiled at Sheila and nodded.

"We agree to your requests."

Sheila heard what sounded like the humming of thousands of bees and then she was in a whirlwind of color. When it stopped she was back in the old meadow with her mother and Gilley.

"Do you think that Patrick is okay? I gather that whoever was after him was after his gold." I asked as soon as I could.

"I'm sure he's fine and waiting for us at home. The who, I'm not sure of, but it doesn't really matter. The King and Queen put a forgetful spell on anyone that recognized Patrick for what he was. So they won't remember him because of that picture," Mother said as they walked over to the cart.

They got into the cart and drove the pony home to the Blarney, with a lot of new stories to tell their clients and put on their site on the Internet.

Shelia looked at her mother and smiled as Gilley pulled out an old stogie and stuck it between his lips.

They were headed home to an exciting future. Father would be able to visit and she would learn about the Fairy; combined with the fixes on the old Blarney and her ideas for marketing, the future was looking very bright indeed.

Party Central

RAMONA SMILED TO HERSELF.

She was going to retire in eight more days. And two days after she retired, she and her husband Wayne were moving to her dream home on a quiet island off the coast of British Columbia. Everything was going exactly as she had planned.

She was a medium-height woman with shoulder length brown hair, grey eyes, and a generous mouth. Her features were pleasing, although a bit ordinary, but when she smiled her face lit up and her enthusiasm shone through her eyes.

Ramona stood by the white, front closet and heard a soft meow. There was the soft bump of a small body against her leg. She looked down to see Susie, her little chocolate Siamese cat. She quickly bent down and gave Susie a quick pat on her pillowy, soft fur.

Ramona grabbed her dark blue wool jacket, her black leather shoulder bag, and the book she was currently reading, and quietly left the small, neat townhouse.

She could smell the tall fir trees that grew in the roundabout at the center of their driveway circle. It was such a strong, refreshing scent she could almost taste it, and tangy scents always put a smile on her face.

She walked the few steps to where her car was parked in its spot directly in front of her home. She paused to look at the rusted-out car parked almost right on the bumper of her car.

She took in a deep breath and tapped the side of her bag with her natural, rounded fingernail as she decided what to do.

Their neighbor Max had parked right behind her again, leaving a huge gap behind him, and now she couldn't get out.

Ramona really detested waking her neighbors, because it was always their young son who answered the door in the mornings while the parents slept in. But she had to get to work.

It didn't seem to matter how many fines they received, Max and his wife still didn't follow the rules.

Although this was one thing Ramona wasn't going to miss.

All the rules in this townhouse complex, and everyone watching everything you do.

She was looking forward to the large piece of property she and Wayne had bought on Goat Island. It was a small island just outside of Vancouver, between the Mainland and Vancouver Island. They would finally have the freedom and the quiet they both craved after living and working in Vancouver all their lives.

It was a mild morning for the middle of February. At six forty-five, the sun had already risen and the increasing breeze was refreshing.

The trees stirred and Ramona heard bird song. She hummed to herself as she walked up to the neighbors' white front door that was identical to hers, except for the number, and the fact that the neighbors' door looked pitted, scarred, and old. She and Wayne had always been careful to take good care of their property.

Ramona knocked on the dented, scratched white door and sighed as she waited for it to open. She didn't want a confrontation, especially today, since she had been in such a good mood. She was happy.

She had started to hum to herself again when suddenly the door opened with a bang.

The smell of stale smoke and stale beer wafted over her. As it entered her mouth, she closed her lips to keep from coughing.

Her stomach rolled and she almost gagged, but she swallowed and managed to stop herself from losing her morning cereal.

Before stood an awful sight.

Her neighbor Max in all his glory: unshaven, unkempt, with his hairy potbelly hanging over his grey striped boxers, scratching his ass, looking down at her. She shuddered as she looked up and kept her eyes fixed on his bloodshot ones to avoid looking at the rest of the man.

"Yeah, what do you want?" Max asked as he belched in her face.

"Your car. Could you move it, please?" asked Ramona, keeping her voice level and trying not to breath too deeply.

She had to focus on the remaining eight days, after which she would leave this place with its looky-loos and its Maxes. That was her goal. Her pot of gold at the end of the rainbow.

Max shook his head, grabbed his car keys off a hook by the door, belched again, and walked out in his stocking feet. He opened the door of his rusty, green, sixty-four Mustang and got in. The old car rumbled to life and he backed up.

Without waiting to thank him, Ramona quickly got into her little red Sunfire and drove to work.

Thankfully they lived close to the office, so she made it for her seven-thirty start time.

She started to shred her soon-to-be-obsolete paperwork first thing in the morning. Her copies of old files and information she had collected from the various jobs that she'd had in the organization. Years of training, information, and work she had done, soon were all gone.

She hummed to herself as she started feeding paper into the machine and watched as little strips of paper came out to fall into the bin.

The air was kept cool in the computer printer room where the shredder was, and soon Ramona was shivering in her light blouse and slacks.

Ramona went back to her small, cramped cubical to get her sweater. She gazed at her plants. She had brought in her own variegated ivy and spider plants.

She'd read somewhere they helped produce oxygen and were helpful in an indoor environment. At first they had done poorly, but she'd brought in a full-spectrum lamp and soon she and the plants seemed to feel better.

Once she finished the shredding for the day, she packed up her light and her plants in the box she had emptied and then took them down to the car park.

She checked her schedule and realized that she had a coffee date with one of her friends, and then another buddy was taking her out to lunch.

She enjoyed some of the attention and she knew that she would miss her friends. Ramona felt her throat tighten at the thought off not seeing her friends again. But they were building a large enough house so that her friends could come visit them on their peaceful island. Many of them had said that they would. In fact she had already booked a few of her friends to come over in the summer time. She was looking forward to that.

***

Ramona pulled up in front of her townhome and stopped short as she saw a children's bicycle behind the bush next to her parking spot. She shook her head.

She parked the car; leaving the engine running, she popped out and moved her neighbors' child's bike, then parked in her designated space.

Ramona knew that she would miss some of the people, but the traffic, the crowds, and the noise, that they could keep.

Although she and Wayne did enjoy hosting and going to parties, she was sure that they could get all that on their little island, too.

They weren't the only people there, after all.

Ramona parked her car and went into her home, ready to tackle another room.

Tonight they were going to clean out the basement and do a real purge on all of their books. She and Wayne were both avid readers and had collected quite a few pocket books. The majority of them had to go. If they were in very good shape, they would sell them, and the remainder they would donate to the local literacy program.

Susie met her at the front door. She quickly gave her a pat and went upstairs to get changed into a pair of soft, comfortable, faded jeans and tee shirt. She then she went back downstairs to take a quick look at how many empty boxes they had in the basement.

The basement had the smell of old paper books and comfortable leather chairs.

"Ramona, I'm home," she heard Wayne call from the main floor above.

"I'm downstairs. We're going to need more boxes."

Ramona climbed the stairs to the main level to give Wayne a quick hug. "Do you want to go and get them or should I?"

"Why don't you get them, and on the way home, stop off at the chicken place and bring home some dinner. I'll start packing up."

Wayne leaned down and kissed Ramona on her lips. Then he rubbed his chin, with its five o'clock stubble, against her soft cheek. She laughed and pushed him away.

Wayne was a man about six feet tall and on the slender side. His hair was beginning to recede but he was still handsome as ever. He was retiring the same day as Ramona, although he didn't seem as excited as she did.

"Eight more sleeps." She gave him another quick hug.

"Yes, dear. We can go over this weekend and take some stuff for the house. I dropped by the builder's office on the way from home and picked up the key. He says it's ready."

Wayne held out the bright new brass key to her as he picked up Susie, who was waiting for her greeting.

"Great, all the utilities kick in starting tomorrow. We'll have heat, and light—everything we need in our new house." Ramona was getting excited.

Susie started to purr loudly as Wayne bent down to pet her soft, sleek fur and scratch her just below her ear—something the cat loved.

"I can hardly wait to see it. We haven't been there since before December, and only the foundation was in then. What if—"

"I'm sure that everything is fine. The subcontractor will meet us at the site. Or should I say our new home." Wayne held up the keys, jangling them in front of Ramona.

She laughed as she pulled on her jacket and picked up her purse. She knew that everything would be fine with their new home. They had had a few glitches along the way, but everything was fine now.

They had rented a van and would take some of their goods over now. Ramona knew exactly what they would need and had already packed the pre-move items.

On the weekend they would take over most of their kitchen. She was also taking along a set of sheets and a new quilt set so that when the bed was moved in, she could quickly make it up. It would give them a nice clean bed to sleep in on their first night in their new home.

Ramona had mapped and measured out where everything was going to go. She had even decided where her plants would be, and had gotten special stands for her rabbits-foot fern and her purple and hot pink bougainvillea.

Not to be outdone, the variegated fichus she had taken cuttings from and propagated at work two years ago was in a pot to take with her.

It was now a nice-sized little tree, and had a lovely, small teak table to call home.

With the southern exposure, they would all do well in the living room, with its cream-colored walls, soft white sheer drapes, and red oak plank hardwood floor. Her special plants would be going with them in this first trip too, while others would come later with the furniture.

It would be a full day. They had reservations and would go over on the first ferry and home on the last.

It was a grey day and sprinkled on the way to the ferry and on the way across to their island.

***

Standing on the ferry deck, she drank in the smell of the salt water and her ears were filled the cries of the grey and white gulls that rode the breeze over the ferry, searching for cast-off food.

For the first time in a long time, she felt her shoulders relax as the stress of her job and the city was released from within her.

As they arrived at their new home, it started to pour with rain.

Ramona was doing her best to sit still.

She was a bundle of nervous excitement and clenched and unclenched her hands as they pulled up the driveway.

The house was just as she had imagined it. The view was breathtaking. Their property overlooked the ocean and the islands beyond, receding toward Vancouver. The emerald green islands looked like stepping stones against the sky blue water.

And the best thing was that they were situated so that no one could build in front of them to obstruct the view.

They had managed to keep most of the tall fir, cedar, and arbutus trees on their property, as well as the native ferns and salal. With the rain it brought out all their natural scents. The air was thick with the scent and sounds of rain and forest.

All of her dreams and plans over the last ten years were about to be fulfilled.

They both opened the car doors, and like two children on Christmas morning, ran toward the house. They stopped to stand under the overhang out of the pelting rain over the front porch of their new home and grinned at each other.

Wayne opened the front door and looked at Ramona. He knew how much this meant to her and how hard she had worked toward this.

"Do you want me to carry you over the threshold?"

She laughed and shook her head. She then took his strong hand in hers, wanting them both to share in the moment. Together they walked through the wide double doors into the foyer.

It was exactly as she had planned. It was beautiful.

The odor of fresh paint and wood surrounded them. She slowly drank it all in. It was perfect.

From the copper-colored tile entry to the grey granite counters in the kitchen and in the bathrooms. The master bedroom, painted a dark cream with white trim, had a two-person soaker tub with a large privacy window so that you could look out at the incredible view while you took a bubble or Jacuzzi bath, and the shower was large enough to have four people in it. It even had a built-in seat.

Wayne went to the attached double-car garage, opened it, and drove the van in. He brought Susie out of her carrier. The cat could wander around the new house and start getting used to the new place.

Soon he and Ramona had everything unloaded from the van.

"Well, honey, we're doing really well unloading. Do you want to go out for a bite of lunch?" asked Wayne as he put away the last glass in the kitchen cupboard.

"What's that noise?" said Ramona as she came from the master bedroom with a bunch of wooden clothes hangers in her hands.

There was a large crash that came from the living room, followed by a loud song with a distinctive Reggae beat.

Ramona looked at Wayne, a quizzical look on her face as if he had the answer to the noise. He just shrugged his shoulders and shook his head.

They followed the noise and discovered in the middle of their beautiful, tranquil living room were an assortment of cats and rats and elephants, all about three feet high, in a long conga line.

The tiny animals were all up on their hind legs, wearing either colorful, long Hawaiian shirts or pants. On their heads they wore white party hats, with bright pink and purple pom-poms on top, and green boas adorned their shoulders.

Susie was walking between them and rubbing against their legs.

"What are you and what are you doing in my house!" yelled Ramona.

They had destroyed her plants and her curtains. Now they were doing a good job in gouging up the hardwood floors.

She quickly ran to the laundry room and grabbed a broom. She raced into the living room and turned off the music after opening the front doors.

Wayne picked up Susie, who had come into the kitchen purring loudly. He put her into the furnace room and closed the door.

"Get out. Get out of my house. Get out now!" Ramona yelled at the top of her voice as she chased the strange things out of the house using the broom alternately as a club or a baseball bat.

They kept on dancing and shouting, "Party! Party!" as they walked past her in a long conga line.

Her ears rang with the noise they made leaving, which almost deafened her.

She went into the kitchen and looked at Wayne, who had gone back to finish putting the coffee cups away.

"Wayne, did you see that?" she said not trusting herself.

"See what? I heard a lot of loud music, but I thought it was just an alarm clock radio that went off." He went and let Susie out of the furnace room.

"No. We just had a bunch of three foot high cats and rats and elephants dancing in our living room," she said.

Wayne looked at her and nodded, but didn't say anything.

She stopped and went into the living room to see if there was any evidence of what she had seen.

Ramona doubted herself. She must have imagined it.

It must be stress.

She took a deep breath to steady herself and opened her eyes. No, the mess in her living room was still there.

She could feel herself start to shake and knew that if she let go, it would be a long time before she could control herself again.

This is crazy. Or I'm going crazy.

"Honey, it's just stuff."

Wayne had come into the living room to stand by her shoulder. "It can always be fixed."

Just then the front doors opened up and the conga line came back into the house and into the living room. Susie joined them.

Ramona went into the kitchen and dragged Wayne back so he could see for himself. The living room had been destroyed. The curtains were torn down, plants destroyed, and the floor was ruined.

Ramona looked at Wayne for an answer and then started to cry. She stopped and wiped her eyes with the back of her hand.

No way was she going to let these creatures ruin her perfect plan. She'd get them out of the house one way or another.

An exterminator. That's what we need.

Ramona quickly picked up the phone and dialed directory assistance. "I need the number of an exterminator."

"That might not be a good idea, Ramona," said Wayne.

Ignoring him she jotted down the number the operator gave and dialed. The phone rang once and a man answered.

"Hi, this is Ramona Fielder at 888 Sunwood Drive. I need an exterminator."

Ramona looked at Wayne, who had joined her, and smiled at him, confident that the problem would go way and then they would clean the house. They could still save their dream.

"What exactly is the problem, ma'am?" came a deep voice over the telephone.

Suddenly, Ramona realized how foolish she would sound asking an exterminator to get rid of the three-foot high cats and rats and elephants from her house. She hung up the phone. She couldn't have the people living on her island thinking she was a loony.

Rita Schulz

Suddenly the music was on again. She looked hopelessly as the conga line wound its way past them. The last one in line passed her. It was a cute Siamese cat who looked exactly like their Susie, except it was three feet tall.

Wayne reached out to grasp one of the cat's legs and gently pulled her out of the line.

"Who are you and what's going on here?" he asked the cat.

"We're from all over the galaxy. This is one of the Party Planets. We come here for our holidays." The cat-like thing stood in front of them with her arms and feet still moving to the beat of the music.

Aliens? Party planets? My new house? "Wayne, do something." Tears streamed down Ramona's cheeks.

"How come we've never seen or heard of you before?"

"The gateway into your house just opened up again. Mars was in the way until recently. But now we can come and party. Your Susie sure is cute and really nice. She says you're really great people and like to party. Want to join us?" Then the cat-like alien ran after the line and quickly joined them again.

The dancers came around again and this time they had the pots and pans out of the cupboards and were banging on them to the beat of the music.

Wayne took Ramona by the hand and led her to the van, opened her door, and made sure she was belted in the passenger side.

"Let's go for lunch. When we come back, we'll see then how everything is. Okay?"

Wayne was right. They needed a break from this madness. What else were they to do? This couldn't be real and it would give them time to think.

Ramona looked at him and slowly nodded her head, letting him take the lead. She wasn't hungry, but time alone with him would do her good.

After a quick light lunch at a local diner, they came back to their new home. They parked in the garage Wayne had forgotten to close, but Ramona didn't say anything.

They went into the kitchen and were met by a purring Susie. Everything thing looked normal and not the mess that had been there when they left.

Ramona and Wayne cautiously entered the living room. There were two grey humanoid beings dressed in plain grey work overalls. One was tall, while the other was shorter. They were working, cleaning up the mess made by the conga line.

And everything was almost back to normal.

One of the aliens was sweeping the floor with a straw broom while the other was putting the final touches on the plants.

The curtains were hung and the floor looked as if no one had ever walked on it before. The house even smelled like no one had ever been there before, all fresh and clean.

The taller alien with the broom spoke as he kept on sweeping.

"Sorry for the mess, but we cleaned it all up. Just out of curiosity, why did you build a home right in the middle of a Travel Gate? You must really like to party."

"How often does this happen?" asked Wayne.

"We come through this destination about once a month," he answered as he stopped sweeping. He pulled out a sheet of paper from his pocket and looked at it. "Yeah, every four weeks on Saturday at 12:00. And we're punctual," he said with obvious pride.

Every month? Oh, no. My peace and quiet.

***

Wayne and Ramona pulled up at their townhouse late that afternoon after a very quiet trip home. Neither of them had said a word to each other. They were each lost in their own thoughts.

Ramona went into their townhouse and sat down on a kitchen chair. She just stared ahead, not seeing anything.

Wayne let Suzie into the house and soon she was weaving between their legs and emitting soft, encouraging meows.

Ramona looked down at her and started to say something, but stopped. What was there to say?

"Honey, we'll think of something," said Wayne, trying to comfort her.

"What can we do? It must be something in the water or the air. It's not real, Wayne. What we saw wasn't real."

"Well…"

"Oh come on, what you read and see on television isn't real. You do know that," said Ramona. She looked at Wayne as if trying to decide if he was just trying to humor her or he was being serious.

"Oh sure, Ramona I know it can't be real, but what if it is?

"I say let's move in like we planned next week and see how it goes."

Ramona slowly nodded.

That's all they could really do, she thought as she could feel herself start to plan again.

The alien said they come by once every four weeks on Saturday at 12:00. Now that gave her something to work with.

***

Ramona's last day and retirement party went as planned. The party was very nice, with good presents and speeches accompanied a few tears. Wayne had a similar send off at his job.

The move had gone well, too.

Ramona had postponed her friends' visits that summer. She told them they were going to have a second honeymoon, and would need a little more time to settle into their new routine.

The fourth Saturday came. The large, polished-brass kitchen wall clock showed 12:05.

There was no sign of the aliens. No music, no conga line, nothing. Ramona started to relax. They'd obviously imagined everything.

Ramona and Wayne sat in their large open kitchen having a late brunch of fresh bran muffins with fruit and finishing off an excellent cup of coffee.

She knew they were safe. She could feel the tension in her body starting to melt way like sun-warmed butter. It had all been their imagination.

"Yes. I know what you're thinking, and I agree. I don't know what came over us that day. All I can think of is that it must have been mass hallucination; well, I guess mass is the wrong word, but you know what I mean." Wayne smiled at her.

She nodded at him. Their life was perfect. It was quiet and ordered. Susie sat with them in the kitchen, waiting too.

Ramona almost spewed a mouthful of coffee across the table when a sudden burst of noise erupted from the living room.

"Now arriving planet Earth. Hoop! Hoop! Party! Party! Party!" They heard yelling and shouting from the living room. Then they heard the blaring of music and they could feel the vibration of many feet stomping on the floor.

"No, it's not possible. It can't be real," cried Ramona as she felt her calmness, her serenity shatter.

They stood up, followed by Susie, and went into the living room. Sure enough, there were the little aliens and the conga line winding its way through their home.

"Well, Ramona what do you think?" Wayne reached out to take her hand in his as she shook her head.

"What are you talking about? This was supposed to be our quite life.

"You know, read some books, go for long walks. Sit on the porch and watch the sunsets," she said as she sniffled.

"Yeah well, we could do that later. Why don't we do a little exploring first? I bet we could see some really interesting sites. And we could always come back to Party Central and sit on the porch when we're ready."

Ramona looked at Wayne, a confused look on her face, thinking about all her planning. Her world had totally changed. But was that necessarily bad? This could be the end of her nice, orderly world. Was she ready to take a chance like this?

She looked into the eyes of her husband and realized that he had never really been completely sold of her dream of "retirement."

Oh, well. When you can't fight 'em, join 'em.

Wayne was right. They could always come back and sit on the porch when they were ready.

The conga line came past them again, only this time Wayne, Ramona, and Susie joined it.

Party time!

A Little Kitchen Magic

LUCY, A PRETTY, SLENDER GIRL IN HER LATE TEENS, stood in the middle of the large, bright, country kitchen leaning on her broom, worrying about Tom, her brother. She hadn't seen him in a very long time, and then it had been only a very short visit.

They lived in the little village of Squamish, which lies in the shadow of the Pacific Coast Mountains, just outside Vancouver. A very small town that lots of people passed by on the Sea to Sky Highway on their way to the resort town of Whistler, but few ever stopped.

"Lucy, you can't do anything about it, so you may as well stop fretting. It happened a long time ago. You know that the odds of turning that boy back into a human after all this time are little to none."

Lucy looked at Nona, a tall, grey-haired woman, the town's friendly wise woman, and smiled at her. Lucy went back to sweeping the old wooden farmhouse floor as she had promised to do, but her mind was firmly set on this problem that her brother had accidently created, and affected her directly.

Their family was cursed to wander the earth. They would never be able to settle anywhere for any length of time.

Tom had accidently turned his best friend Cory into a werewolf, and Cory had in turn cursed the family. Now the only way to fix everything was to cure Cory. Simple. At least Lucy thought so.

"I know that, but is there anything else that can be done? It's not like Tom meant to hurt his friend and turn him into a werewolf. He actually did his friend a favor. It was a case of him dying or drinking the potion. And he chose…"

"Stop it, Lucy! That's enough. The University judged him, found him guilty, and now his fate is sealed. He'll wander all his life and never find rest," said Nona. Her voice was sad, but firm, as she peeled a batch of potatoes for dinner.

Nona was as frustrated as Lucy, but she couldn't let the young girl know that.

What Nona didn't say was that Lucy would have the same fate: to wander as her brother when she got older, since the curse was on Tom and his family. Their parents were dead and it hadn't affected Nona, at least not yet.

Nona wasn't sure when Lucy would start to wander, and kept a sharp eye on her. She had striven to prepare the girl as best she could.

"I know, but I do miss him."

"Me, too. I can't help but think that he would have made a great wizard, but something really went wrong."

Nona went out into the backyard to work in her garden, leaving Lucy to finish her chores.

There was a ring of the doorbell. Lucy went to open the front door. She was surprised to see the UPS man in his brown uniform, with a package tucked under his arm.

"Mrs. Thompson?" he asked. He smiled at Lucy with a slightly wolfish grin. His large brown eyes scanned around the room. Finally his eyes settled on Lucy.

Lucy looked up at the tall, dark-haired man and smiled at him, too.

He certainly wasn't hard on the eyes, being your typically tall, dark, and handsome male type.

"I'll call Nona for you," said Lucy.

"No worries. Tell you what; I'll just leave the package for your grandmother—it's her little book, Kitchen Magic—and take you with me," said the man as he dropped the old, faded, dark blue book on the coffee table and swept Lucy up into his arms. One hand covered her mouth and the other held her firmly around the waist.

Lucy realized that this wasn't a delivery person it was Cory, who must have taken Nona's book.

Lucy heard her Nona call to her as she was swept out the door. She tried to yell, but she couldn't with the man's hand so tightly held against her mouth.

She struggled and tried to kick him, then she tried to use her elbows, but he was too strong and held her tight.

Fear rose in her belly and her heart beat hard against her chest. He carried her out of the door, down the path to his idling truck. The only thing to do was to bite him hard, as hard as she could, so he would drop her.

She drew back her lips and opened her mouth as wide as she could. She knew that she would only get one chance at this.

"Don't try it, Lucy. I'm Cory. The man your brother turned into a werewolf. If you bite me, we don't know what my blood will do to you.

"It could turn you into a werewolf, too. Don't forget I was turned by magic."

She was shocked and stopped fighting. His voice was low and guttural, almost like a vicious dog's snarl as he spoke.

He quickly tied her up, gagged her, and threw her into the back of the truck.

Lucy tried to think of some way of escaping and not of what would happen next to her, but her mind went there anyway.

She pulled against her bonds, trying to get her hands and feet loose, but nothing would give. She was tied too well. She focused on trying to loosen the ropes; she wouldn't give up.

Was he going to kill her? But if that was what he wanted, he could have done that already. She thought of different possible solutions, finally realizing that all she could do was wait and see. She knew that she would find a way out of this situation—she had to.

It was a long drive, but the twists and turns were familiar to her. Soon they were out past Whistler, then they turned onto a little-used gravel back road that even Lucy wasn't familiar with. It seemed to her that her body was being shaken apart with all the ruts and potholes the truck hit. She fell asleep.

She found herself waking up when the shaking and the crunch of gravel under the tires stopped.

She woke confused and disorientated. She tried to stretch her legs, but when she couldn't move, she remembered where she was and that she was tied up. Fear bubbled to the surface inside of her.

It was late afternoon, almost dusk. She knew that night would be falling soon since it was getting dark in the truck.

She wondered if Cory would turn into a wolf tonight.

The back of the truck opened up and there he stood. She waited until he got closer and tried to kick him with her bound legs. He just stepped to one side and smiled at her.

She was afraid of him.

She reminded herself he was a killer. That's what werewolves were. Natural killers.

He picked her up as if she weighed nothing, put her over his shoulder, and carried her inside a small cottage. The drapes were drawn and it was dark. He carried her into the living room and dropped her onto the couch. It was a rough old red thing that scratched her cheek and smelled like wet dog.

Lucy let out a small exclamation as the air rushed out of her lungs.

How dare he drop me like an old sack of potatoes?

She heard him rattle around in the kitchen and smelt wood smoke. Then his heavy footsteps came back into the living room.

"Lucy, listen to me," he said and turned his back to her.

She felt something cold and hard touch her ankle, and then she heard a soft click. She tensed at the sound. What had he done to her?

She craned her head to see what was happening, but couldn't see anything because his body blocked her view.

His strong hands grabbed her under her armpits and pulled her into a sitting position. She saw that she now had a metal ring around her ankle, attached to a long chain that was anchored to the floor.

Lucy's mouth went dry with fear and she realized he was planning to keep her captive for a long time.

"Lucy, I'm going to untie you now, but as you see, you can't get away. And there aren't any neighbors for about five miles, so no one will hear you scream. All you're going to do is hurt yourself if you try."

As Cory said this, he untied her ankles and wrists and finally he remove the duct tape from her mouth. It ripped her skin and her eyes teared up, but she refused to let it show.

She was determined to maintain her outward control.

"What do you want with me? You've already cursed my family. What more do you want?"

"It's getting late so we'll have to talk about that tomorrow. Right now you need to know a few things. The chain you have around you ankle is very strong and very long. There is a small shed at the back of the cottage and I need you to lock me into it. This is for your own safety. You will let me out in the morning because I have the keys to the truck and the supplies, which are out of your reach. Without food and water you will die."

"Why are you doing this?"

She watched him closely and one of her questions was being answered. She saw his eyes start to grow larger, rounder and a deeper brown.

"Quickly, this is your one key for the shed. Follow me," he said as he handed her a new brass key.

Lucy got up, fighting the pins and needles in her legs and arms, and followed him as quickly as she could.

There was a small, new outbuilding behind the cottage and out of sight from the road. It looked sturdy and was made of heavy timbers. It only had one door in the front.

There was a small barred window beside the door.

"I need you to lock me into the Kennel. Quickly now, it's getting dark."

Cory opened the door, turned, and closed it.

Lucy stood at the door. The chain on her ankle was tight but it had reached its end.

She smiled at Cory and locked him into the building, then stepped back.

She now had all the power.

Twilight had come and the sky had turned a dark orange, then a deep purple as the stars appeared in the clear sky.

"Sleep well, Lucy," said the werewolf as the last part of his humanness faded. He became a wolf.

There was another, larger outbuilding on the other side of the house, one she couldn't reach, just like the truck that was parked too far for her to get to.

Lucy went back into the house and smelled hot stew. Her stomach growled. She realized that he had heated the stew for her supper. The smell made her mouth water and she realized how hungry she was.

The cottage had two large bedrooms. One was empty and the second had a large bed in it.

Lucy was petrified. She had to find a way out of this place before morning.

She got up and headed for the wood box that she had seen at the back of the cottage next to the kitchen door; she hoped that she would find an axe. It was empty except for a good supply of chopped wood.

Next she searched through all the cupboards and drawers in the kitchen. She looked for anything that she could use as a tool to help her get the iron ring out of the floor or the metal bracelet off her ankle. All that she found were some pots, pans, and spoons.

She made a quick but thorough check of the closets and any other area that may hide any tools. Nothing.

She started to shiver and realized that the cabin was getting cold now that the sun had disappeared and went to start a fire in the fireplace. There was a fire all laid out and ready for her. Soon she has a nice warm fire. She picked up the wood poker to move the logs over and her heart jumped as she looked at the poker. This might be her answer.

She quickly went over to the ring in the floor and realized that the handle was too wide to fit the ring and the other end of the poker was too wide, too. Neither end would fit into the ring.

Lucy realized that if she used the bottom of the poker, she might be able to use it as a pivot point to pull up and loosen the ring. It worked.

She still has a very long length of chain attached to her ankle, but she was free.

Lucy knew that she was miles away from anyone, but if she stayed on the roads she was confident that she would come across someone.

The moon was bright and it helped as she walked down the gravel road. Around her owls hooted on the hunt and the tress rustled in the cool breeze.

Then she heard a heavy, pacing sound in the bushes and quickened her pace. Lucy heard it again and then stopped. The sound stopped as well.

Lucy started walking again and felt a set of eyes were on her. She heard the yowl of a large cat. Was she being hunted? She heard it again. The sound seemed closer. She finally panicked and broke into a run.

She looked behind her. There in the moonlight was a large cougar. It lifted its muzzle into the air and started toward Lucy again. It was getting closer.

Then she heard the snarl of a wolf close by. The sound terrified her, but for some reason also made her feel hopeful.

She left the road and took cover behind a wide old evergreen next to a large clump of rocks.

She watched the wolf attack the cougar. Lucy rooted for the wolf. She hoped he didn't get hurt.

The cat attacked quickly and tried to claw the wolf's belly. The wolf twisted just in time to avoid the lethal strike and turned to grab the cat's neck from behind and shook it hard.

The wolf was much larger and heavier than the cat, and the cat realized it. The cat made another attempt, but gave up what it thought was an easy meal, turned, and ran into the woods.

At first Lucy was happy the wolf won, but soon her feelings turn cold as the wolf turned and walked slowly toward her. He snarled, his razor-like fangs showing clearly, his head hung low, his yellow eyes studying her.

Was this Cory, the werewolf, or was this a wild wolf on the hunt for a meal?

She looked around for something to defend herself with and only found a handful of small, loose rocks. She gathered them up.

The wolf approached her. Fear coursed through her body making her hands wet with perspiration.

Am I going to die now?

She forced herself to keep breathing, to keep staring down the wolf, to face her fear. She gripped the rocks tightly, ready to throw them.

As the wolf grew closer it stopped and changed into a man.

Her fear ebbed and she realized she was holding the rocks so tightly that they were cutting into her palms. Since it hurt, she dropped the sharp stones and came out from her hiding place.

"You lied to me," said Lucy as she wiped her wet, gritty hands on her jeans. "There was another way out of the Kennel."

"Good thing for you there was. Come on," he said and started to walk with an easy stride back to the cottage. He seemed casual and confident in his own skin.

"You can change your shape when you want to? You're not governed by the moon?"

He shrugged his shoulders but didn't answer.

The gravel road was rough and she had to make sure that she didn't step in any large potholes.

"My brother made a mistake. There must be something you can do to reverse the potion's effects," said Lucy, her voice soft in the night air.

Cory snorted, a soft sound, and shook his head. "Do you think I'm stupid and haven't tried? I've gone to the University, to my own doctor, and anyone else that I could think of. No one could help me."

Lucy sighed; she felt stupid and bad for Cory. But she held on to her belief that someone could help him.

"What was my brother using when he tried to cure you?"

"What do you mean?"

"What spell or potions book was he using? Something from you classes?"

They finally got to the cottage and went in. Lucy hadn't realized how cold it was outside and started to shiver. She wasn't sure if it was from the cold outside or if it was a delayed reaction to everything that she had gone through that day.

She sat down on the couch. "Well? Was it one of the books from your courses or from somewhere else?"

"It was an old, faded, dark blue book that he ran and got," he said as he went into the second bedroom. He came out a few minutes later, barefoot and wearing a pair of old blue jeans and a black tee shirt.

"I know what we need to do," said Lucy as she watched Cory lean down and throw another log onto the fire.

She watched him and waited until he looked at her. She knew that she would need his undivided attention.

"What, you know of a good witch doctor for me to see?"

"No, you need to see Nona and Tom," she said.

She suddenly realized that she really wanted to help Cory.

He had cursed her family, but she still wanted to help him.

"It sounds like it was Nona's old spell book Kitchen Magic that Tom was using, and if he made a mistake, then maybe they can work on figuring it out."

"I'm not going to repeat myself. Nothing is going to help me."

"Look, before you get all defensive, it's worth a try," she said as quickly as she could.

Lucy looked him right in the eyes, waiting for him to react and get angry.

She had never been more afraid in her life, not for herself, but that he would refuse to get help.

Cory's shoulders dropped and she knew that she had won, at least this first round.

"Why did you bring me here?"

"Why not? I'm tired of living in isolation."

"Is that why you brought me here? Because you're afraid of hurting someone as a wolf?"

He didn't answer her, but came over and unlocked the ring around her ankle.

He quietly turned and went out the back door, turned into a wolf, and ran into the dark woods.

Lucy closed the door behind him.

She sat on the couch, exhausted, but her mind wouldn't rest as it went over everything that had happened to her today. As well as everything she had remembered about the story, the mistake her brother had made, and the curse on the family.

She was sure that if she could get everyone to Nona's, they would be able to fix this.

**

The morning dawned bright and the blue jays in the evergreens woke her.

She sat up and realized that she had fallen asleep on the couch and had a bad crick in her neck.

She could hear someone in the kitchen and the smell and sizzle of bacon. She felt her stomach rumbled with hunger pangs. The smell of freshly brewed coffee filled the cottage and she smiled to herself. She could get used to someone making her breakfast in the mornings.

She went into the kitchen and sat down on one of the old oak chairs behind the large wooden table.

She felt good and positive this morning. She knew that she was on the right track in getting Cory fixed and the curse off their family.

Cory put a plate of bacon, eggs, and toast in front of her and sat down next to her.

They quickly filled their plates and both started to eat.

"Lucy, I'm going to take you back home this morning," said Cory as he bit off and chewed a piece of toast.

Lucy nodded silently as she took a bite of her eggs and waited for him to continue.

She waited, but he didn't say anything more. She felt confused, but thought that it was wisest not to say anything right now. This wasn't the right time or place.

They left right after breakfast; the ride was long, but quiet. It seemed that both of them were deep in their own thoughts.

They finally arrived in front of Nona's home and she got out. She turned to wait for Cory, but he stayed in the truck.

She went around to his side of the truck and he rolled down his window. She looked into his deep warm brown eyes and smiled.

"I'm not coming in with you. I've taken the curse off. You and your family are free from it."

"Why? Why don't you want to come in? I'm sure that Nona could help you," said Lucy.

She heard desperation creep into her voice and stopped herself.

Lucy knew that she should be happy that the curse was off her family, and she was, but it wasn't enough. She also wanted to help Cory.

The front door of the house opened and before she knew it Tom and Nona both hugged her.

Tom looked at Cory.

"I'm sorry," said Tom.

Cory nodded.

"Come into the house please, Cory," said Nona.

Cory sat there and looked at them and shook his head.

"I've taken the curse off your family."

"We know. Thank you. Now please come in. I think we have something for you as well."

"Actually I have been thinking about it and I've decided to stay the way I am, at least for right now. Can I get a rain check if I decide to change my mind?" asked Cory smiling.

Lucy was confused. She thought that he would want to be human again.

But he hadn't attacked her last night, so maybe he didn't need to live in isolation any longer.

Perhaps he finally realized that he wouldn't hurt anyone after all, and that it was only his fear of himself that kept him in isolation.

Then she realized he was human and could take on the wolf form whenever he wanted to.

Maybe now he did have the best of both worlds.

Also available from 53rd Street Publishing

In the year 4444 and a 1/4 the Lushites have returned.

Piper Cleaner, First Assistant to the Assistant Surveillance Officer, discovers a Lushite intergalactic vessel heading their way. Alarm bells ring throughout the galaxy!

Have the Lushites returned to seek revenge?

Join Piper and Major Virginia Slim on a crazy, outrageous ride across the galaxy in the far future where addictions are rampant and conspiracies thrive.

The second book in War of the Lushites series is a satirical space opera revealing the future of addiction.

Available in an electronic edition for $6.99.

Amazon, B&N, iTunes, Kobo, Smashwords and others.

It is also available in trade paperback from Amazon and other book retailers